The Third Prophecy

AHMED ESSOP

The Third Prophecy

PICADOR AFRICA

First published 2004 by Picador Africa
an imprint of Pan Macmillan South Africa
P.O. Box 411717, Craighall, Johannesburg 2024
www.panmacmillan.co.za

ISBN 0-9584708-6-3

Typeset in 11 on 15pt Palatino by PH Setting
Cover design by Donald Hill of Graphicor

Printed and bound in South Africa by CTP Book Printers

For Yusuf Garda, Hussain Savant and Yussuf Nazeer

Life's but a walking shadow, a poor player
That struts and frets his hour upon the stage,
And then is heard no more.
Macbeth, William Shakespeare

l

TWO HUNDRED GUESTS WERE seated in the sumptuous dining-hall of the Midas Hotel in Hyde Park, a Johannesburg suburb. They had been invited by the Minister of Education, Dr Salman Khan, to celebrate two special occasions: his sixtieth birthday as well as the fifth anniversary of the transition from the Apartheid era. The guests comprised business executives, bankers, magnates of international commercial corporations, chancellors of universities, school principals, rectors of colleges, government officials, members of parliament and Cabinet Ministers. The only Indian present was Mr Khamsin, an extremely affluent merchant who was a member of parliament. Mr Khamsin lived in the same suburb as Dr Salman Khan, in the former exclusive white suburb of Houghton. There were other Indians in parliament, but he had not invited them as none of them, he felt, measured up to his academic eminence. Many years before, Dr Salman Khan, after graduating with a Bachelor of Arts degree, had left the country to pursue further studies at Cambridge University and later had been appointed professor of Medieval History at the same university. He had lived in England for over three decades, had been chairman of the Socialist Party of South Africa, and had taken part in many demonstrations against the racist regime of his country of origin.

When he returned during the reconciliation period that followed the surrender of power by the patrician class to the inhabitants they had formerly oppressed, he had been approached by the African Front, the leading resistance movement, to join the Reconciliation Congress that had been established to chart the future of the country. When transition occurred with the holding of democratic elections, he was included in the Cabinet for having made an outstanding contribution to the liberation struggle during his exile, and during the negotiations that were a prelude to the transfer of authority.

When Dr Salman Khan and his wife Elizabeth arrived in their chauffeur-driven Mercedes Benz, they were met at the entrance of the hotel by the managing director. As they entered the dining-hall the guests stood up and applauded.

Dr Salman Khan was dressed in a dark grey suit. He was of average height, his physique tending to diminish in muscularity with age. His receding, soft hair was brown, wavy and streaked with grey, his eyes blue and his face pale so that in appearance he looked more European than Eastern. His wife was a woman whose figure had filled out since her arrival as there were many banquets to attend during local and international conferences. She had not been an attractive woman when Salman married her, nor had she attended a school where the arts of feminine grace and deportment were taught. The other women guests wore designer garments, and they had visited hairdressers and the salons of beauticians that morning.

A small rostrum had been erected in the corner of the hall for the Minister to address the guests. The managing director, a tall suave man, welcomed them:

'Ladies and gentlemen, the management of Midas Hotel is honoured by the presence of the Minister of Education, Dr Salman Khan, and all the distinguished guests present here this evening. I hope that the menu will come up to expectations. The Minister will now address you.'

He went over to the rostrum, the managing director adjusted the microphone for him and he said:

'Ladies and gentlemen, I am grateful that you have accepted my invitation to be present here this evening, not only to celebrate my birthday, but also the fifth anniversary of transition to democracy from racist totalitarian rule. Some of us may see this evening's celebration as a happy coincidence of two events and others as a decree of destiny. I have in my capacity as Minister of Education done everything in my power

2

to redress the damage done by repressive Apartheid education that relegated the proletariat to be hewers of wood and drawers of water. I have, as you are all aware, not only deconstructed the academic terminology of Apartheid learning, but altered the structural racist academic establishments to conform with multi-national criteria.

'You will all concur when I say that the portfolios of Education and Health are the pre-eminent ones of state administration. The mental and physical well-being of citizens is of paramount importance if there is to be progress in any direction. I can say with some pride that there has been a renascence in learning. I will not elaborate further. You are intelligent men and women and cognisant of the achievements of our democracy since transition. What I want you to consider this evening are the contributions of exiles who left South Africa when repression became intolerable. They left a country where evil flourished and the difference between fair and foul unknown. They pursued the quest for freedom in foreign lands. They were not impotent exiles living off charity and seeking entertainment always, as some Opposition members in parliament and some journalists have alleged. I have remained and will always remain on the side of the dispossessed in the world. I am grieved to say that my people in this country, the Indians, after transition, have turned their backs, with the exception of a minority, to the formerly dispossessed indigenous majority that is struggling to free itself from the enduring traces of the Apartheid legacy. Many have regrettably allied themselves with the previous holders of power who are in parliament and continue to obstruct the way forward for the empowerment of the proletariat.

'One of the great achievements of our democracy is that it is absolutely secular. Religion, which I regard as a delusion imposed on humanity by impostors, is now banished from within the national parliamentary legislature as well as from every state institution.'

He paused, for a moment and then concluded: 'Ladies and gentlemen, I thank you again for your presence this evening.' There was applause.

Mr Khamsin rose from his seat, went to the rostrum and said: 'On behalf of everyone present, I wish to congratulate Dr Salman Khan on his sixtieth birthday anniversary. May he have many more birthdays to celebrate.'

There was applause.

The managing director then called upon the Honourable Minister of Finance, Mr Delanie, to address the guests. He took a goblet of wine, went to the rostrum, congratulated Dr Salman Khan for having lived through six decades and added:

'Since his Cabinet appointment, Dr Khan has exerted himself diligently in his portfolio to display to the former white rulers that he could excel them in the post assigned to him. He also wished to fulfill the confidence placed in him by the President who, unfortunately, cannot be present with us this evening as he is out of the country on an official visit. I have no doubt in my mind that a man whose birthday coincides with the fifth anniversary of the first democratic election after nearly four hundred years of misrule is destined to achieve great things for our country.'

There was applause.

'Ladies and gentlemen, take your glasses ... To Dr Salman Khan.'

The glasses were emptied and they sang the usual song.

Dinner was served by waitresses wearing tight black skirts, cream blouses and short white embroidered aprons. Afterwards the guests had tea or coffee and delicacies while they were entertained by a singer. Later, in an adjoining ballroom, there was dancing. Others indulged in conversation.

Mr Khamsin, a tall portly figure who changed his seven hand-tailored suits every year, sat at the same table as Dr Salman Khan. He had once sported a neatly groomed beard but had shaved it after his appointment to parliament as he felt that it would not be consonant with his new status. The two men had become firm friends. They often travelled together by airbus to Cape Town, the legislative capital of the state since the days of Apartheid. They visited each other during week-ends and during recess.

'Salman,' Mr Khamsin said, 'was it wise to have mentioned Indians who do not support our party. Your speech will be in the newspapers tomorrow.'

'I thought over that for many days, but finally decided to include what I said. They must be told the truth, for soon the President will announce the date of the next election.'

'You think they will vote for the party?'

'If they do not the consequences can be serious. The proletariat may come to think that Indians betrayed them by voting for predominantly white parties.'

'How can they. Many were involved in the liberation struggle and some gave their lives.'

'You must understand, Ismail, that future generations may not remember that. In fact they may not remember my part in the struggle.'

'Then we must do everything we can to win our people over in the coming election.'

Elizabeth did not comment on the discussion the two men were engaged in as she was enjoying the delicacies the waitresses were offering and speaking to Mrs Amina Khamsin who was dressed in a red sari edged with gold filigree.

The director of a mining company came to congratulate Salman on his speech, and later Mr Delanie, a close friend of Mr Khamsin, came over to join them. He had been responsible for Mr Khamsin's appointment to parliament after a seat had become vacant on the death of a member.

Salman and Elizabeth said goodnight to the guests in the foyer, and when the last guest had left, they thanked the managing director for having provided an excellent menu and said that they would recommend the Midas Hotel to others.

II

A MONTH AFTER DR SALMAN KHAN'S sixtieth birthday celebration at the Midas Hotel, the President announced the date for the second general election which would be on the same basis of proportional representation as the first one. All political parties would be given two months for preparation and electioneering among the citizens.

The African Front, having received the largest percentage of government financial allowance since it commanded the majority of seats in parliament, braced itself to retain its leadership and, if possible, obtain two-thirds of the votes by reducing public support for other parties. Salman and Mr Khamsin appeared on many platforms, several times in the company of the President, lauding the achievements of their party, and promising the citizens that many new homes would be built in the future so that the squalid settlements on the periphery of cities would no longer exist; that tap water would be provided in rural areas; many new clinics and schools established; hospital services improved and pensions raised.

The news media was soon involved with the forthcoming election. There were articles, discussions, debates, on what had been achieved by the administration and what not. There were accusations of maladministration and proud statements of progress and future prosperity. Political commentators and analysts gave their views.

Two weeks before the election Salman was asked to participate in a televised panel discussion with three others: Shareef Suhail, a historian, essayist, literary critic, former member of parliament and former political prisoner on Dragon Island during the repressive era; Mr Ayer, the Consul of India; and Mr Roma, a well-known scholar of African traditions, social commentator and faith healer.

Millions of citizens heard the views of the four men. Shareef Suhail predicted that there would be a significant shift in voter support from the African Front to other parties as the new emerging middle-class in urban areas was disillusioned by the ruling party's performance on social issues, especially the failure to curb crime; the Indian Consul praised the economic and cultural links between the two countries and stated that his government had, after independence from British colonial rule, supported the African Front militarily and financially in its struggle against white domination; Salman stated that the country had seen what his party had achieved in the field of education, and that its continued interest 'in this primary facet of civilisation was part of the renascence process', and that the administration would 'rededicate itself in the future to the achievement of prosperity'. Mr Roma, who was not dressed in a suit like the others, but in a long maroon robe with an embroidered white pattern along the neckline, said that as long as moral values embedded in African heritage and traditions, in universal religious wisdom, were absent in the vocabulary of politicians whose philosophy was largely materialistic in content, a fully civilised social order would not be created. He mentioned that incalculable psychological and social damage was being done by the many 'casino palaces' and the introduction of the state lottery that further impoverished the poor, enriched a few, and promoted instinctual greed.

Discussion followed. Salman pointed out to Mr Roma that the cumulative funds derived from the lottery would be used for social reconstruction. He was supported by Mr Ayer, but Shareef Suhail contended that there was no certainty that the bureaucracy involved in distributing the funds would not be corrupt as this was a common failing of officials everywhere in the world when dealing with public funds. Other issues raised during the discussion were the manufacturing of weapons and their export to unstable states, the entry of international criminals who brought addictive drugs into the country, infrastructural collapse, and hopes unfulfilled. Towards the end Mr Roma uttered three prophecies:

'I predict, firstly, that a star will soon set in the political firmament. Secondly, that this country is going to pass through a dark phase in the coming years. And thirdly, that there will be a recovery when a Muslim becomes the president.'

The prophecies concluded the discussion. As they were unexpected and seemed not to be in accord with the issues discussed, no one commented.

When Salman reached home the third prophecy mushroomed in his mind. A Muslim president! A Muslim to be the president of a secular state? What did Mr Roma, a faith healer and probably a dabbler in witchcraft, know about Islam? There could be several explanations for his prophecy. Perhaps he had been paid to make it by some fundamentalist Muslim sect; or he had received a large sum of money from a charitable trust and wished to display his gratitude by the pronouncement; or some unscrupulous divines might have convinced him that the future president would be a Muslim; or he expected to be rewarded by some Islamic missionary organisation. His disquisition about moral values was the usual stock-in-trade of priests and Sunday preachers on television and in stadia. His prognostication that a star would soon set was that of a gypsy crystal-gazer in a caravan. What star? There was nothing profound in that. As for his prophecy about the coming of a dark phase, that was a platitude that charlatans were fond of making to the credulous. He wondered who, among the directors of the national television station, could have invited an impostor to discuss political matters.

Salman did not think of the prophecies again. He had many public meetings to attend. The President selected him to be at his side when he addressed meetings in the main cities. He was extremely pleased as he was exposed to the attention of the news media. Mr Khamsin said to him:

'I think the President is grooming you to take his place one day.'

'Why me?'

'Why not? He is giving you credit above all Ministers as being the most competent.'

'Ismail, do you seriously think so? We are a small minority in this country.'

'Mr Roma, during the panel discussion on television, prophesied that a Muslim would be president in the future. Do you recall?'

'That cuts me out. You know I am an atheist.'

'You may revert to Islam.'

'No, never. I am a firm Marxist.'

'What the Almighty decides, will happen. He can change our views even if we resist.'

'I don't believe in the myth of a Creator.'

'Believe what you wish, but only the Almighty determines human destiny.'

Salman gave no further thought to the conversation.

Electioneering came to an end. On a Sunday, the last day before the citizens of the country went to the polling-stations, the President made a special appearance on television during news time in the evening and said to the nation:

'I have decided not to stand for the presidency again. I have served my people long enough during the liberation struggle and during the negotiations with the white regime that led to the transfer of political power to the African majority. What I had wished to see as a young man, when I worked in a gold mine on the Reef, has now been achieved, a democracy where all South Africans are equal in status. I am deeply grateful to the comrades who stood by me during the years of oppression and during my exile in Russia. I wish the citizens of the country peace and prosperity. Farewell.'

Salman reacted with astonishment to the statement. He had been very close to the President during the past few weeks, and he had not even hinted at his intention to resign. He had addressed vast crowds in stadia and had been honoured by dancers, traditional praise-singers and applauded over and over again, ensuring victory for the party. Was this an impulsive decision? He was a prudent man who made decisions after careful judgment. There had been no consultation with the Cabinet or his compatriots who had been in the struggle with him. Did he wish to make a dramatic retreat from politics so that the impress of his resignation would affect everyone profoundly and that future generations would speak about it?

He said to Elizabeth, 'Did you expect him to make this announcement on the eve of election day?'

'No, but politicians act capriciously at times.'

'The President is not known for that. I can't fathom why he has stepped down.'

'Well, the way is now open for the new president. Do you think the Vice-President will take over?'

'I cannot say who will be chosen.'

'He enjoys much support from party members, though you accompanied the President to mass meetings more times than he did. Perhaps he was intimating his choice for the presidency.'

'Mr Khamsin also says so. But the black majority will not accept me at present. Perhaps in years to come.'

'Well, wait until then.'

Salman telephoned Mr Khamsin, several Ministers and members of parliament to hear their responses. They expressed shock and bewilderment. Some felt the President had slighted them by not taking them into his confidence. They deserved some respect for having struggled together to achieve the new political dispensation.

Salman could not fall asleep that night. He went to the kitchen, took a glass of fruit juice and went to sit on the rear balcony of his mansion overlooking the swimming pool. While taking a sip he looked up at the sky and saw Jupiter shining brightly below the belt of Orion and the prophecy of Mr Roma flashed through his mind. The star! Yes! A star would set. The President had set. It came to him like a revelation. The man had spoken the truth. There was no doubt. Prophets spoke in symbolic language. Nostradamus.

He rushed to the bedroom and woke his wife.

'Elizabeth, Elizabeth, what the prophet predicted has come true. A star has set.'

'What star?'

'Elizabeth, listen to me. The prophet predicted that the President would step down.'

'The prophet?'

'Yes. Mr Roma. The man in the robe. Don't you remember the televised discussion when I appeared with him?'

'Yes.'

'Didn't you hear him predict that a star would soon set?'

'Surely you don't believe he meant the President?'

'I am certain he did. Prophets speak in riddles.'

'Salman, don't set your mind on this. If you said this at a party meeting they would call you a lunatic. Prophets belong to the past.'

Rationality reasserted itself.

'You are right. I should not become superstitious. Prophets have always deceived their disciples by referring to heavenly bodies.'

'You should sleep now.'

'I will come to bed soon.'

He returned to the balcony. Jupiter shone in a cloudless sky and transfixed his eyes with its brilliance.

On election day, in the evening, Mr Khamsin and three Ministers living in the same suburb, came over to Salman's home to discuss the new situation that had arisen after the President's resignation.

'I have spoken to the Vice-President,' Mr Delanie said. 'He is annoyed. There was no consultation.'

'Why has he done this?' Salman inquired.

No one said a word for a while.

'It is as though a meteor had come from outer space and shaken the earth,' Mr Khamsin said imaginatively.

'His resignation will go down in history,' Mr Tero asserted.

'There must be a reason,' Salman insisted. 'He is known for his forethought and consideration for others.'

'Sometimes,' Mr Khamsin declared, 'an outside influence controls decisions.'

'Ismail, I know what you are going to say next. God.'

'No, an angel.'

There was amusement.

'You believe in angels?' Mr Muso asked.

'The theologian at the Mayfair Mosque told me that there are angels who direct human affairs and who am I to disagree with him. He spent ten years at Al-Azhar University in Cairo studying religion.'

'Perhaps a psychologist may have an explanation,' Mr Delanie suggested.

'Maybe it's political fatigue,' Mr Tero speculated. 'We seek profound explanations when there are none.'

'Your opinion would be valid,' Salman replied, 'if he was a simple man. I have examined history for precedents, but can find none.'

'Salman,' Mr Khamsin said, 'I think the explanation resides with the choice of the man who accompanied him to mass meetings. You. He wanted to tell the nation who should be his successor.'

'No, that cannot be.'

'What do the others think?'

There was no comment.

Two servants came in with tea and trays of refreshments. The President was forgotten and they talked of victory at the polls and the parties that would be held in celebration.

'We must go to the Midas again,' Mr Delanie said.

'Yes,' Salman agreed.

'And who will pay?' Mr Muso inquired.

'Leave that to me,' Mr Khamsin said. 'The hotel received much publicity after Salman's birthday celebration. I will speak to the managing director.'

'Yes, we must celebrate in grand style,' Mr Delanie concluded. 'Victories don't come every day.'

III

THE ELECTION RESULTS WERE announced after a week. The African Front retained its supremacy, though suffering a reduction in votes in several major cities. The Vice-President, Mr Zara, was elected as head of state and Mr Delanie succeeded him.

Mr Zara was a tall austere-looking man always dressed in imported suits, white shirts, expensive cufflinks and tie pins. He was clean shaven with hair never out of trim. His ring finger was ornamented with an onyx. In 1960 he had left the country on an exit permit (offered by the white regime to its opponents to seek permanent exile) for America. There he had set up his headquarters to gain support for the destruction of the racist patricians. He received aid, financial and moral, from African-Americans, took part in protest demonstrations, spoke to White House officials and the President, associated with diplomats, and addressed the United Nations Organisation in New York. When the time for reconciliation (initiated by the former President) with the white rulers arrived, he returned to his native country.

Mr Zara was formally inducted within the precincts of The Castle, originally built as a fort in the seventeenth century by Van Riebeeck, the first commander of the Dutch settlement at the Cape. Thousands of foreign dignitaries were invited: ambassadors, princes, presidents and prime ministers from the East and the West, and several monarchs. There was banqueting and dancing.

The vast sum of money spent on the induction displeased Salman and Elizabeth.

'I could have had five schools built or a university,' he said in the evening at home.

'It heralds a dark phase.'

'Dark phase did you say?'

'Yes, a dark phase, indeed. A man who spends so much public money on his inauguration will plunge the country into decay.'

'He does not show much concern for the poor.'

'We shall see how he performs.'

'Yes, the testing time has now arrived for him.'

'I hope he retains you in the Education portfolio.'

'You mentioned a dark phase, Elizabeth. Mr Roma predicted that a star would set and a dark phase would follow.'

'That's star-gazing nonsense,' she said, taking a newspaper and beginning to read.

Salman felt agitated, uncertain of his future. He stood up and went to the balcony and looked up at the sky. Radiant Jupiter stood above a bank of dark clouds. Macbeth's soliloquy sprouted in his mind:

> Two truths are told,
> As happy prologues to the swelling act
> Of the imperial theme.

Macbeth had been his prescribed matriculation text for study at the high school he attended in the inner-city Johannesburg Indian suburb of Fordsburg. He had memorised many extracts from the play as the English teacher said that examiners were always impressed if the answer to an essay question was buttressed with relevant quotations. He had also taken the part of Banquo in a dramatic performance in the school hall. He was murdered by the hirelings of Macbeth. The play had etched itself on his memory. In London he had seen two stage productions and in a cinema in Cambridge two screen versions.

When parliament reconvened in Cape Town President Zara announced the Ministers of the new Cabinet. Two former Ministers were dropped and the portfolios of others shifted. The Ministers of Health and Justice were given the portfolios of Transport and Environment respectively, and the Minister of Education transferred to the Prison Services portfolio.

When Salman heard of his transfer he sat, petrified with humiliation, during the rest of the session that lasted over an hour. The parliamentary chamber and all the members seemed to contract in his vision as though he were in Lilliput. He was no longer aware of the proceedings, a lonely withdrawn figure. He awoke to reality when he felt a hand placed on his shoulder.

'We must go now,' Mr Khamsin said.

He rose and followed in a trance. Outside, a limousine arrived to take them to their hotel. He did not comment in the car on what he considered to be a calculated reduction of his status by the President. He felt imprisoned in a moving cell, even when Mr Khamsin tried to console him by saying:

'I am pleased that you have been retained in the Cabinet.'

At the Diaz Hotel they sat in the lounge. After drinking some ice-cold water Salman emerged from his despondency to converse.

'I have been demoted.'

'No. President Zara, you must understand, is a secretive man whose thoughts no one can penetrate. He calculates every move he makes.'

'Like a good chess player?'

'Yes. He may have felt that you established the ground work in education and the new Minister could now continue to build on what you achieved. He needs you now to reform the prison services that require, as you know, much attention. The prisons are flooded with inmates, some have escaped, and officials are not performing well. I am sure that was his thinking.'

Salman was grateful to his friend for the explanation.

During the night he slept fitfully. He felt his being reduced, negated. He had fallen from zenith to nadir. In parliament he would no longer command the respect he had enjoyed. He blamed not the new President, but the former. He had used him during the election period and then discarded him. He should have exercised his authority and instructed President Zara to retain him in his portfolio.

Salman had met the former President many times in London when he came over from Russia to address public meetings called by the Socialist Party. On several occasions he had stayed at his home in Cambridge. Now he would live in his palatial mansion in East London and forget him while he, Salman, walked in rank dark prisons among thieves, bandits, rapists and homicides. His memory swelled with Macbeth's words before the entrance of the three professional murderers:

> Light thickens, and the crow
> Makes wing to the rooky wood;
> Good things of day begin to droop and drowse,
> While night's black agents to their preys do rouse.

On Saturday morning Salman and Mr Khamsin returned to Johannesburg by airbus.

When Salman reached home Elizabeth was not in. She usually spent mornings assisting a private welfare organisation in a poor settlement on the periphery of the city. He sat in the lounge and read the *Saturday Chronicle* which he had bought at the airport. The editorial dealt with the appointment of the new President and speculated on his ability to steer the country during the next half decade. There was an assessment of the new Ministers, their competency to fulfill their responsibilities, and there was this comment:

'What is noteworthy in the Cabinet changes is that two former Dragon Island political prisoners have been dropped, and that Dr Salman Khan has been shifted to the Prison Services portfolio. His transfer, after having received much praise for his sterling accomplishment in the field of education is, to say the least, mystifying.'

The comment pleased Salman. When Elizabeth arrived they had lunch and later went to have tea in the gazebo near the swimming pool. She said to him:

'I am afraid you are not going to find President Zara easy to work with. He seems a conceited, morose man.'

'I have known that for the past five years.'

'You will go through a dark phase, walk in corridors, underground passageways, dungeons.'

Salman looked at his wife and had the transient illusion that he had not seen her before, never known her. Those were not her words, but that of another being. Corridors. Underground passageways. Dungeons. Could there be some link with the prophecies of Mr Roma? There was something occult going on.

'The prisons are on the surface, Elizabeth,' he said in a subdued voice. 'There are no medieval dungeons.'

'He has humiliated you.'

'Yes. I must resign.'

'Why should you? There is the salary to consider.'

'Salary?'

'We need money to live. Do what you have to do, even if you don't like the work. The next election will be on a constituency basis and you could be defeated.'

'Elizabeth, you mentioned that I would go through a dark phase. The prophet Mr Roma said that the country would experience a dark phase.'

'Surely there is no connection between my words and his. The phrase is a commonly used stereotype. Besides, the Prophet Muhammad was the last. I have heard of no one after him.'

'That' s true,' Salman concurred, standing up from the wrought iron chair and going towards the pool. He looked into the water and the fear of drowning came over him.

'I will take a walk,' he said to himself. He walked along a pathway and then sat on a bench near a small pond where a black gargoyle vomited water. He reflected on the change that had come to his life. The five previous happy years had vanished forever. They had been part of the 'new dispensation', a phrase that had often been uttered by the former President who was now as good as dead, having abandoned him to the dictatorship of his successor … to live in obscurity, carrying the burden of his fall … deliberate act to humiliate, did not attend celebration in Midas, family commitments, excuse spurious,

18

fled into exile, did not resist iron reign of aristocrats, jealous of academic status, must cease speculating on future, poison thought and action, Elizabeth right, salary, realistic, carry on next half decade, not wilt, show mettle, rise from dungeon darkness.

Salman spent the next day reading the voluminous Sunday newspapers. There were articles by journalists, political analysts, academics, special correspondents, evaluating the period since transition and predicting the future in the political, economic and social spheres. Some writers were hopeful as they felt that the new President was a 'realist' who perceived that the country could not dispense with the help of the Western world and its democratic institutions. Extracts from his past speeches were reproduced to support their argument. Others were full of despair, pointing to the collapse of the infrastructure in various parts of the country, the inordinately high crime rate, the corrupt bureaucracy, the lack of responsibility shown by some Ministers. There were brief biographies of the new Ministers, and speculation on how they were likely to perform in their posts. The *Sunday Express* contained two articles by well-known novelists assessing the past since transition and predicting the future. One wrote of the 'manifold substantial achievements of the multi-national democratic administration under the renowned President during the past five years after the destruction of the racist Apartheid regime', and the other maintained that 'the once wealthiest state on the continent of Africa is declining into a slough'. After reading the newspapers Salman decided to count the articles that were optimistic about the future and those that were pessimistic and found that the former exceeded the latter by five.

IV

D URING THE NEXT SIX MONTHS Salman devoted himself to his work. He was assisted by specialist consultants – according to innovative administrative practice, they were engaged to assist Ministers in their portfolios – so that he could receive all the advice he needed to run prisons efficiently. He requested reports from all the provincial prison administrators and studied them. When administrators were lax he did not hesitate to send strongly worded faxes to them. He went overseas by plane to various European countries to familiarise himself with prison conditions and regulations and learnt how they dealt with recalcitrant inmates and what rehabilitation facilities existed. The prison population in the country was increasing rapidly. There were the youth who emerged from school, found no employment and descended into crime; and there were the professional criminals, gangsters, drug-dealers, serial rapists, hijackers, murderers. There were thousands of awaiting-trial prisoners crowded in jails as the justice system could not process them speedily enough. He approached the Construction Ministry and requested that more prisons should be built. The reply he received was that there was insufficient finance and the Ministry was 'burdened with other priorities'. He decided to inform the President of the situation and requested a meeting.

As soon as he entered the President's office he was told that he should be as brief as possible as an American Congress delegation was expected to arrive soon. Salman spoke of overcrowded prisons, the strain on administrative staff, and presented various statistics.

'Yes, yes,' the President interrupted, 'that's enough. You should consider finding other accommodation. There must be many empty state buildings somewhere. Seek and you shall find.'

'They may not be suitable for prisons and may require reconstruction.'

'Professor, you have been given the responsibility to act. Consult your consultants. We can't go on paying them for sitting around. Give me a written report some time later.'

He walked out of the office, riled by the President's curt manner. He realised he was going to be faced with many problems. When he told Mr Khamsin of the interview, he advised him not to take umbrage at the President's approach as his international commitments left him little time to give his attention to home affairs.

He felt depressed. He told Elizabeth of the interview.

'Why should you be upset? A suggestion has been made by him. Write to the Housing Ministry. Perhaps there are empty state buildings that can be converted into prisons. You should know by now that governing a country such as this one is not easy. You know its history.'

'Yes, but why must I implement what is unprecedented, utilise empty buildings as prisons. Even if the Justice Ministry approves, I will be held responsible if things go wrong.'

'You can defend yourself by saying the idea came from the President.'

'I suppose so,' he said miserably. The President had humiliated him by deposing him from the Education Ministry and now was intent on crushing him. Macbeth's words erupted in his memory:

O! Full of scorpions is my mind, dear wife.

'Salman, when you come home do not bring your problems with you. Forget them. If you go on in this way you will crack up. Let us go out for lunch today and then to the cinema.'

V

Yusuf Ebrahim, a former member of parliament who had lost his seat as support for his party, the People's Movement, had been severely reduced during the election to three representatives and as a consequence had been left out, entered Salman's office after making an appointment with his secretary, Allison Mercer. He was a lean man with sparse curly grey hair, jutting cheek-bones and a wrinkle-lined forehead.

'Dr Khan,' he said, I need your assistance. I intend resigning from the People's Movement and joining the Front.'

'Is it because you lost your seat?'

'No. I think the Front is the only party representing the true aspirations of the people, and all other parties are driven by ambitious individuals who want to stop the empowerment of the proletariat.'

'You must speak to the President.'

'He may not want to see me. You know that at times when I was in parliament I was very critical of the administration.'

'Then I am presented with a difficulty. Why don't you write a letter to him stating your reasons for leaving the People's Movement. I am sure he will consider.'

'A personal approach by you on my behalf would be better.'

'You want to join the ruling party. Is that all you want?'

'Understand my position, Dr Khan. I was in parliament for five years. Now I am out. I shall be glad to be appointed ambassador or consul in some Arab country, Egypt, Tunisia or Libya.'

'Why in those countries?'

'I spent many years there as an exile, mobilising support for the destruction of the white regime. I know many heads of states and the people. I don't want to be in limbo.'

'Alright,' Salman responded, 'I will speak to the Vice-President.'

22

The loss of his parliamentary seat, though not equal to his own humiliating transfer, made Salman feel sympathetic.

'Thanks very much.'

'This is what I suggest you do. You have the status of a former member of parliament. Go to a newspaper and tell the editor that you have decided to leave your party and intend joining the Front. He can phone me for a comment.'

Mr Ebrahim went to the offices of *The Cape Herald*. The evening edition of the paper reported that an important official of the People's Movement, and former member of the legislature, had decided to defect from his party and join the African Front. There was a brief history of the part he had played in the liberation struggle and during his exile in the Middle East where he had found sanctuary after his flight. His photograph was prominently displayed and Salman was quoted as saying that everyone had the democratic right to leave one party and join another.

Salman did not speak to the Vice-President. He decided to get Mr Khamsin's advice first.

'Do not ask anyone in the administration to find a post for Mr Ebrahim. The man has defected from his party. He cannot be trusted. He may abandon our party after the next election. He is an opportunist.'

'I feel sorry for him.'

'That sentiment must not enter politics. You must not compromise your position. Tell him to make an appointment with the President himself.'

When Ebrahim came again Salman told him that since he had received publicity in the press he could now approach the President personally and make his request for a post in the foreign service.

Ebrahim frowned and left.

He came again after a week. He told Salman that the secretary of the President had informed him that he was too busy to see him at the present time.

'Mr Ebrahim, I advised you to write a letter.'

'If you approach him personally I have a better chance.'

'Mr Ebrahim, that is impossible. In fact you have to be formally accepted into the party. I cannot do that, only he can.'

'You have the standing and influence that no other Cabinet Minister has.'

'Why don't you apply for a post in the civil service in the meantime. There are many vacancies.'

'I will not do that. I was a member of the legislature. You want to demote me.'

'No. I thought that perhaps some employment might help in the interim period until a diplomatic post becomes available.'

'It is that and nothing else.'

'Then there is not much I can do for you.'

Ebrahim left, looking very agitated. Salman felt sorry for him, but he remembered Mr Khamsin's advice.

He came again after a month. He was now looking haggard and desperate.

Salman said to him: 'Mr Ebrahim, why don't you think of doing something else until the next election. Everything is going to change then. Elections will be based on constituencies and not proportional representation. You will certainly be elected.'

'I can do nothing else.'

'Have you no vocation in life? Surely you must have done something before seeking exile.'

'Politics is my vocation. You made me resign from my party and now refuse to do anything for me. I am in limbo. Limbo! You understand!'

'Mr Ebrahim, if I was responsible for appointments in the foreign service, I would give you a post right now. Made you an ambassador to Egypt.'

'Ambassador? Did you say ambassador, doctor?'

He laughed loudly.

'You are now my prisoner,' he said standing up. 'You double-dealer!'

He laughed again.

Salman stood up. He feared that the man was demented and could attack him.

Allison opened the office door.

'You,' Ebrahim said, pointing an accusing finger, 'are now my prisoner, Minister of Prisons.'

He chuckled.

Allison left the office quickly to summon the orderlies.

Ebrahim moved to the left of the desk and Salman took a few steps away.

'So, you infidel, you refuse to help me.'

Salman looked at his hands. Was he going to draw a knife or a gun?

'Let me tell you this. You have not long to live. I will send you to hell where you will be embalmed with fire.'

'I promise I will speak to the President.'

'Promise did you say? Today will be your last. You are my prisoner, Minister of Prisons.'

He laughed hysterically, lifting his arms up to the ceiling.

Three orderlies rushed into the office, grabbed hold of Ebrahim and dragged him out of the office while he screamed, 'Minister, I will imprison you on Table Mountain, near hell, you ...'

'I should have kept him out,' Allison regretted.

'It's not your fault. He lost his seat in parliament and cannot accept it.'

VI

ONE DAY, MR BENGALI made an appointment with Salman in his office. He was a man who had not said a word to him within the chambers of parliament building or outside, over the years. He was always dressed in a white cotton shirt that reached his ankles and an embroidered white skull cap. His beard was black and long. He was an outlandish figure in the council chamber of legislators wearing suits. He was said to have been a former principal of a religious seminary. Why he had been appointed by the African Front, nor what part he had played in the liberation struggle, no one seemed to know. There were eight other Indians, besides Mr Khamsin, in parliament, but Salman had refrained from becoming friendly with them. Mr Khamsin was an exception, for he was not only an extremely wealthy man, owning many shops and wholesale emporiums, but a pleasant personality who had acquired a store of worldly wisdom.

Mr Bengali came into the office and sitting down said:

'Several members of a Muslim organisation approached me and asked me to arrange a meeting with you at your residence in Houghton.'

'What do they wish to see me about?'

'I said to them that you would not wish to speak to them on religious matters as you are an atheist.'

'Why did you presume that I would not wish to meet them? And did I tell you that I am an atheist?'

'I have been told that you are a follower of Karl Marx.'

'Who told you?'

'I cannot remember.'

'Is a Marxist ipso facto an atheist?'

Mr Bengali did not answer. He looked up at the ceiling. Then he said, 'I have made a mistake.'

'A serious faux pas.'

'I apologise, Professor Khan.'

The apology made Salman less brittle.

'Well, what do they wish to consult me about?'

'They belong to a missionary society and wish to speak to you about religious activity in prisons.'

'Did you not inform them that ours is a secular administration and that religious propagation is not permitted.'

'I did not. I thought if the professor would tell them it would be better. You understand my position.'

Mr Bengali belonged to a puritanical sect. Salman had seen members of the sect dressed like him in the streets, sometimes with their wives in black robes and veils.

'I will see them on Sunday afternoon at three.'

'Thanks very much,' he said and departed.

Four men came on Sunday, dressed like Mr Bengali and bearded. They sat down in the lounge and a very pale man, his veins visible along his temples, said that they had come to inquire whether they could obtain permission from his Ministry to undertake missionary work in prisons so that criminals would come to realise their sins, repent and later become good citizens.

'I am afraid we do not allow religion to be propagated in state institutions.'

'We want to help prisoners to lead a better life.'

'You mean you want to convert them?'

'No, we want to give them advice.'

'You mean preach morality?'

'No.'

'What then?'

'Only advice.'

'What you want to do is to make converts.'

'Yes, professor,' a corpulent man said.

'But that cannot be allowed.'

'Why not?' another man demanded. He was the tallest of the deputation and looked fierce. 'You are depriving us of our democratic rights.'

'Who told you that?'

27

'My lawyer.'

'Why did he not come with you since he knows so much about your rights?'

The man remained silent.

'Gentlemen,' Salman said in a softer tone, 'there is no way I can concede to your wishes even if I want to.'

'We were allowed in Apartheid times,' the pale man said.

'That time has passed.'

'We know that,' the tall man said. 'You come from overseas and you make laws against us.'

'I suppose that is also what your bright lawyer told you. I have not made laws against you. There is an Act of parliament.'

'What parliament? Most of the time members are sleeping.'

'It is obvious that you are ignorant about state administration, including your clever lawyer.'

'Why do you have a Muslim name? You don't believe in God.'

Salman rose in anger.

'Parliament, including Mr Bengali, voted for a state that will not promote religions. Go and consult your lawyer. You will soon get an account from him for his clever advice. Get out!'

They looked at each other, rose and left. 'Fanatics!' Salman said as Elizabeth came in.

'Why are you angry?'

He told her of their request.

'Ismail would have handled them tactfully.'

'Yes, I should have called him.'

During the evening his anger with the deputation shifted and fixed itself on Mr Bengali. Knowing the law against proselitisation, he had shrewdly used it to embarrass and insult him. Now he was their friend while he, Salman, was the enemy, not only of the four delegates but their entire organisation.

On Monday, in the council chamber, Salman turned to look at Mr Bengali sitting far behind him. The man looked as impassive as always. Salman saw him now as a sinister figure.

28

He never skipped a session, never said a word, and voted obediently when required to do so.

At supper time in Diaz Hotel Salman told Mr Khamsin of Mr Bengali and the deputation's visit.

'You should have sent them to me. They belong to a very strict sect.'

'Elizabeth said you would have handled them diplomatically.'

'In future refer religious organisations to me.'

'I will. You know I have no time for believers.'

'I am one,' Mr Khamsin said, raising a glass of orange juice to his lips.

'You are not a fanatic.'

'Of course not. In life one must make compromises. Take this lesson from me. If you are not a believer never proclaim it. You know what happened to Salman Rushdie.'

'They accused me of being an atheist.'

'There are times when God works in ways we cannot understand. He may make you an outsider so that you may come to see the value of religion in a clearer way.' Salman smiled.

'Ismail, your views are always interesting. You will remain an optimist always.'

'I believe that it is better to speak of a half-full glass of liquid than a half-empty glass.'

'That sums up your philosophy very well. I shall now drink orange juice from a half-full glass.'

Salman could not forgive Mr Bengali who, knowing that the request of the missionaries could not be granted, yet sent them to him. He had primed them to insult him and diminish his dignity. Only he could have told them he was an atheist and the 'lawyer' who was their advisor was probably none other than Mr Bengali himself. Whenever Salman entered the assembly chamber and glanced at the bearded face of his adversary he felt a wound festering within him. He decided to visit the Minister of Safety and Security, Mr Durrel, in his office.

'Come in, come in, doctor. I am very pleased to see you. When we meet each other in the assembly chamber or in the dining-hall there are always others. We have four hundred and sixty representatives and I am told that is the highest figure in the world. Now what can I order for you? Tea? Coffee?'

'Thanks very much, but nothing today.'

Mr Durrel was a bloated man with a small face and spikey grey hair. He had belonged to the outlawed Communist Party during the previous era, had been imprisoned several times, thereafter managed to escape by bribing a warder, then fled to Zambia where he spent many years organising the resistance movement.

Salman told him of Mr Bengali, how he had come with a request to meet four men belonging to a fundamentalist sect, the conversation that ensued, emphasising and expanding what they said about members of parliament sleeping in the assembly chamber, and the insolent attitude they had displayed towards him.

'I believe he is a dangerous man. He used me cunningly to interview fanatics who wish to undermine the state.'

'Yes. He should have told them himself.'

'Have you noticed his dress. Always the same, a discordant figure. He is an ambitious man and may have secret designs.'

'Yes, invariably dressed in the same garb.'

'I think you should keep him under surveillance.'

'I will inform our Intelligence Agency. We keep a watchful eye on all those we suspect want to damage our young democracy.'

'Do you know that he has not yet said a word in parliament since his appointment. He must be the highest paid legislator in the world for his silent contribution.'

'Or for lifting his hand when voting,' Mr Durrel added.

'I am sure you appreciate that an attack on one Minister is an attack on all.'

'Don't worry, professor. You know the motto of the Three Musketeers, "We are one for all, and all for one." If we discover Mr Bengali supporting conspirators we shall use our swords.'

'Thank you very much Mr Durrel.'

The Minister shook Salman's hand and opened the door for him.

VII

SALMAN, BEFORE WRITING A report on conditions in prisons in the country, visited several in the Cape Province and then decided to visit the largest penitentiary in the remote northern part of the country. The superintendent had informed him that the buildings designed for three thousand inmates held seven thousand. He had read reports in newspapers of 'unacceptable conditions' prevailing there. It was necessary for him to visit the penitentiary to see for himself, and also to pre-empt criticism of his Ministry for its indifference.

He asked his Deputy Minister, Mr Dudu, to accompany him. They went by plane and landed at the airport near the city of Pietersburg where they were met by the Provincial Administrator. They went in his limousine to the penitentiary a few kilometres outside the city.

The superintendent was waiting for them and they were led inside into a labyrinth of passages, corridors, barred cells, steam-filled kitchens, dormitories, dining halls, ablution blocks with malodorous smells. Salman was overwhelmed by the thousands of faces staring at him. He was informed that many were awaiting-trial inmates who could not afford to pay bail in the courts. The endless rows of cells, the incessant noise, the clang of opening and closing steel doors reminded Salman of dungeons in Europe during the era of Inquisitions.

'We must do something to improve conditions,' he said to his Deputy as they walked along. He did not comment, he showed no interest, as though the prisoners were animals of the same species in a zoo. He was bored. Salman questioned many prisoners, inquired about their crimes, the length of their sentences, if they had sufficient food, whether family members visited them, whether fellow prisoners stole their belongings or maltreated them. He opened cupboards and looked inside. In the kitchens he examined the food being prepared, spoke to the chefs and mentally recorded everything he saw and heard.

He was pleased to find the women's section of the prison in a better state. There was no overcrowding. He found the women sewing, knitting, making bead adornments, and babies being cared for by their mothers. There was laughter and a pleasant atmosphere.

In the superintendent's office he asked many questions and made notes. He also questioned the provincial Administrator. How often did he visit the prison? Did he speak to the inmates? Did he have a record of complaints?

In the hotel, while his deputy sat in the lounge drinking liquor, he wrote the report for the President in cursive.

Next morning they took the plane back to Cape Town. Salman handed his written report to Allison to type and deliver to the President.

After three weeks Salman and his deputy were summoned to the office of the President.

'I have looked at your report. What are you doing about the conditions?'

'We need to build more prisons to ameliorate conditions. Provincial administrations do not have sufficient funds.'

'Nor does the state.'

'Sir, if the courts were more stringent in imposing harsher sentences on offenders, we would have a reduction of prisoners.'

'You should think of releasing certain categories of prisoners.'

'Releasing?'

'What else? You tell me.'

'I will have to consult the Justice Minister.'

'Do so. I do not wish to read in newspapers that nothing has been done.'

He returned to his office and asked his deputy what he thought of the President's proposal. He smiled and said:

'You must decide. You are ultimately responsible.'

The press, having heard of the Minister's visit to the penitentiary, inquired what steps were being taken by the administration to improve conditions. Salman issued the following statement:

'My perception of the reconstruction of prison services is underpinned and inspired by practical considerations other than theoretical subjective analysis that will deliver a framework capable of being formulated and supported by existing budgetary constraints and resources, and the availability of finance from extra-governmental sectors. A further press release will be made after decisions are considered, ratified and finalised.'

Salman asked Mr Khamsin what he thought of the President's suggestion of releasing prisoners.

'A good idea. Free the awaiting trial prisoners who have committed minor crimes.'

'Without any conditions?'

'Let them report to the nearest police station every week until they are summoned to appear in court.'

'That's a good idea.'

'To ease the pressure further let the administrators grant parole to those who are well-behaved.'

'That sounds reasonable.'

'Prisoners who have served ten years or more should have their prison sentences cut by a quarter. And the courts should sentence those who have committed minor crimes to house arrest. That will save the state money to care for them.'

'Ismail, you have all the answers. But will the Justice Ministry agree.'

'See the Minister of Justice and tell him that the President has instructed you to make proposals to his Ministry and that these should be implemented.'

Salman's proposals were accepted and put into practice. There was criticism from Opposition members of parliament and from editors of newspapers. Some predicted a collapse of the justice system; others argued that the released prisoners, if they had been employed before their incarceration, would now find themselves without work and descend into further crime. He responded by stating that though the action taken by his department in collaboration with the Ministry of Justice was

34

unprecedented it would 'ameliorate a situation that poses a dire threat to good governance and civic stability.'

Salman was riled by the criticism. Mr Khamsin told him that that was to be expected: 'Critics do not have the foresight to see that improvements as a result of administrative decisions do not occur instantly. In a few months' time they will see the difference and praise you.'

In spite of Mr Khamsin's assurance, Salman felt imprisoned in a medieval underworld. He could not forget his fall from the heights of the Education portfolio. He saw himself in the midst of thousands of criminals crushed in rank-smelling dormitories and cells, distracted by incessant noise, leered at by murderers, rapists and sodomites. He yearned for the luminous days when he was welcomed by chancellors of universities, rectors of colleges, and garlanded by school principals at assemblies. He had been honoured by teachers' organisations, invited to conferences, photographed, presented on television, and lauded by the past President. He had now fallen from meridian heights into 'dungeon darkness', a phrase that recurred in his consciousness with searing dismal finality.

VIII

SALMAN'S FALL FROM THE Education portfolio, his humiliating experience with Mr Ebrahim in his office, his visit to the penitentiary, made him feel that he was being drawn into the 'dark phase' of Mr Roma's prophecy. He wondered whether his professorship of Medieval History at Cambridge had in some way determined his fall. Would he eventually be swept into the gloom and be heard of no more? Or would he regain the eminent position he once held?

What would be his future in politics? If the third prophecy came to fruition would the Muslim president consider him for an appointment?

On his way home by car with Mr Khamsin from the airport he had seen two gypsy caravans at a road intersection with a banner attached to two poles proclaiming in purple letters: Your True Future Told by Fortune Queens. Driven by his search for certainty and tempted by the enchanting term 'queens' he decided to visit them. Perhaps they possessed supernatural knowledge. One Saturday afternoon while Elizabeth was away visiting friends, he drove along the highway that led to the caravans.

As he drove along he considered whether his desire to know the future was wise.

If the prediction was made that he would be killed by criminals would his days and nights not be poisoned by fear? Or if he was told that he would attain fame as a great statesman, would that not lead to complacence, inaction and culminate in failure. Ambition was the motive force in any endeavour to attain fulfillment. Then there was the possibility that the prediction might be enigmatic so that he would have to rack his mind to discover its meaning, and only when disaster struck would he come to know the truth.

While all these thoughts were passing through his mind, the car reached the intersection where the caravans were parked.

Trepidation seized him. There was no certainty that the gypsies were not criminals in disguise. He drove on and stopped a short distance away. Should he return home or 'screw' his 'courage to the sticking place' and visit the 'queens'?

Of course they could not be criminals as the caravans were stationed in a public area, and permission must have been granted by a provincial authority to conduct their business. Would they tell him the truth or weave fantastical lies to take his money? Was he lily-livered and afraid to face crystal-gazers? He had come a long way. He turned the car and went towards the caravans.

He parked his car and emerged. He saw no one. He walked around the caravans, noted that they were new, large and probably the most expensive of the Luxline brand name. The curtains were drawn and he could not see within. He tapped at a door. There was no answer. He was returning to his car when a door opened and a melodious voice cried:

'Don't go way, sir. We here.'

She stood in the doorway, a slender woman in a long floral skirt, with a partly exposed midriff, a tight blouse, a pink scarf tied to her head, wearing earrings of two intertwined silver circlets. Her wrists were ornamented with coloured enamel bangles. She smiled at him, beckoned with a ruby-flashing finger and he went towards her.

He entered the caravan and saw two other women, dressed in identical fashion as the one who had called him, sitting at a table. Incense from burning joss sticks floated above them.

'Please sit, sir. We tell good fortune, me my sisters.'

She sat down opposite him. 'We all queens. Make nice love, like in movies.'

He looked embarrassed. They laughed.

There was a crystal ball in the middle of the table and playing cards lay strewn all over. He noticed that there was a complete hand of cards lying in an arc before him.

'Now, sir, what you want to know?'

He looked at her in surprise. He had not come there to be questioned but to be told his fortune.

'I want to know my future.'

'You have good future. Lots money in bank.'

She had noted his Mercedes Benz.

'I don't want to know about money.'

'We know everything happen to you. Even today.'

'Tell me.'

'You sleep with me first.'

'No.'

'With we three.'

'No.'

They laughed at his embarrassment.

'Alright. Your future very good. See cards before you. All say good fortune come to you.'

He looked at the cards. He was not a fool. They were placed there permanently. He began to regret that he had come.

'Look into crystal. Think of nothing. We three also look and tell fortune after.'

He looked at the crystal ball for what seemed to him an inordinate length of time, during which his mind strayed to his youth when he stood before a gypsy tent gaudily painted with signs of the zodiac at the Rand Exhibition in Milner Park. He had been afraid to enter, but two of his friends went in and came out laughing. He could not remember what they said. His memory evoked Macbeth's and Banquo's' encounter with the witches on the heath and Banquo's address to them.

> If you can look into the seeds of time,
> And say which grain will grow and which will not,
> Speak then to me, who neither beg nor fear
> Your favours nor your hate.

The 'queen' facing him clapped her hands. 'Now we tell fortune. I first. You get big brown box with ribbon with many boxes inside same.' The gypsy on his right said, 'You look and find big hole.' The one on his left said, 'Your photo in newspapers.'

'Now I explain,' the 'queen' said, looking into the crystal. 'First, you marry big brown woman and have many children. Two, you see big hole in desert. You find steps go down to palace. You enter and become king. Three. Your photo in houses in country. You lead happy life with much money in bank.'

The three women pointed their fingers heavily laden with rings at him.

'Now you pay three queens who tell good fortune three hundred.'

'I can only pay one.'

'No. You pay three. Or I call police. We got cellphone. And we curse.

You make accident.'

The three woman laughed at him and stood up. The thought occurred to him that they had daggers concealed in their garments. They could stab him, throw him out and disappear with his car and caravans. He paid quickly.

'Now you pay for sleeping with us.'

'I did not.'

'We offer. Your fault. You pay.'

'No.'

They surrounded him and put their arms tightly around him.

'Sleep with us or pay three hundred.'

He paid.

They went out with him and blew kisses as he drove away.

As he drove home he thought of the prophecies. The first one that he would marry a big brown woman. God forbid. Not Madam Nomsa. How did the gypsy know about her? She was the one woman in parliament that most men feared to cross in debate. Would he be able to escape her embrace? The second one about the hole in the desert and the subterranean palace where he would be king was an Arabian Nights' fantasy.

Aladdin. There was some truth in the last one. It portended fame. And what did that mean? That one day he would be President? No. His photograph had appeared in many newspapers and the gypsies might have seen it.

When he reached home and saw Elizabeth he wondered why he had not told the fortune queens that he was a married man. Would Elizabeth leave him?

He looked at her several times closely and listened intently to her when she spoke to detect any intimation that she would divorce him some day.

Later, after supper, he sat beside Elizabeth in the lounge and watched on television a performance of the ballet *Giselle* by a visiting Russian troupe. He thought of the gypsies. They were not sybils, but women who travelled through many countries, enjoying their lives, preying on the credulous, who were legion, and telling fanciful fortunes. His visit to them was an insignificant episode in his life.

IX

AFTER THE PASSAGE OF several months the city of Cape Town experienced an upheaval among its citizens. An organisation called Unity Movement Against Crime (UMAC), consisting largely of Muslims, began a campaign of opposition to the many gangs in the city and its environs. There were said to be ten major gangs and many smaller ones comprising unemployed youth. They were not only involved in internecine battles and violent crime, but the leaders of these gangs were said to control the drug trade. Some of the leaders were brazen enough to be interviewed on television. UMAC began a series of protest marches in the city, calling on the police to take action. Later they marched with a banner to Parliament Building to present a petition to the President urging him to clean the city of criminal gangs. They also marched to the homes of well-known 'drug lords', some of them Muslims, and pleaded with them to stop trafficking in narcotics. Many who took part in the demonstrations, men and women, covered their faces with scarves as they did not wish to expose their identities to gangsters. Soon a series of shootings began in the city and a number of deaths occurred. A confrontation that led to four gangsters being fatally shot and three civilians, one a child, seriously injured in the cross-fire, led to widespread public concern. Soon prostitutes were murdered and bombs were placed in bars frequented by gays. Motor cars exploded, shattering nearby buildings. The Minister of Police blamed UMAC for initiating the disorder and the Defence Force was brought in to restore calm. But the killings continued. UMAC blamed the police as being in the pay of mobsters. The President accused UMAC as consisting of 'terrorists against democracy and the transition process'. He went on to say further:

'This is an organisation that is determined to establish a fundamentalist Islamic state. It claims that it is combating crime.

It is the state's duty to combat crime, not a religious movement's. It is obvious that they have a secret agenda. That agenda embraces the destruction of the sovereignty of our democratic state. In fact these very people, of Indian and Indonesian origin, voted during the second general election for the predominantly white racist parties, who are now in the ranks of the Opposition in parliament and against transformation. They are always critical of government attempts to redress the wrongs of the past.'

Mr Khamsin advised Salman:

'Keep quiet. Do not enter into the crisis, comment or make allegations. Leave that to others. No one can predict how it will end.'

'The situation is very serious,' Salman concurred.

'We Muslims in parliament find ourselves in a predicament. We are part of the administration and we are also a part of the Muslim community. We have to be extremely cautious in whatever we say or do.'

'Silence can be interpreted as betrayal by the administration and by the community.'

'You are right. But I think we must not commit ourselves to either side at this stage.'

Salman realised that this was the appropriate time to brand Mr Bengali as a fundamentalist. He could not forgive the man for having sent the missionaries to him and being insulted by them. He telephoned the head of the Intelligence Agency and said to him:

'Listen, Colonel Van der Ray, I have received information that a member of parliament, Mr Bengali, is sympathetic towards the fundamentalist terrorists who are causing havoc in Cape Town. Perhaps you should keep him under surveillance.'

'Doctor, we have already done so. We are not sleeping.'

'You already have?'

'Yes. We protect those who support the authorities, we keep under surveillance those we suspect, and expose traitors and anarchists. Mr Durrel informed me about him some time back.'

'Thanks very much, Colonel.'

'Keep us informed if you know of others.'

A Cabinet meeting was convened by the President to examine the crisis. The following document was presented to the Ministers:

REPORT ON THE ORGANISATION:
UNITY MOVEMENT AGAINST CRIME

The Unity Movement Against Crime (hereinafter referred to as UMAC) was established on 10 April 1999 at a clandestine meeting held in the home of the President, Saleem Anwar Sayid, with the ostensible purpose of contesting criminal gangs in the Cape Province. The meeting was attended by well-known Islamic fundamentalists (as mentioned in Annexure A) and the following officials were elected to serve on the command structure of the organisation: Saleem Anwar Sayid (President), Yusuf Deen (Secretary), Achmet de Vos (Assistant Secretary), Kahlil Hassen (Treasurer). A Working Committee of five others was elected:S. Shafik, M. Ally, D. Fortune, G. Dawood and S. Sarlie.

Since the formation of UMAC the city of Cape Town has witnessed the escalation of crime to an unprecedented level. Many mysterious murders have occurred unrelated to periodic rivalry for domination in the gang world.

UMAC has conducted various protest marches through the streets of Cape Town, and against the consulates of two foreign states, Israel and India. It is an ardent supporter of the militant faction of the Palestinian Freedom Vanguard and the Iranian Revolution. Its choice of targets amply shows that its contest against gangs is a smoke-screen to conceal its true intent. It is a radical fundamentalist organisation that is determined to make the state ungovernable, create anarchy, and wrest power to establish an Islamic state on the basis of Shariah law. That is uncontestably its principal motive. UMAC's appeal to fundamentalist values and theological paradigms should be seen in a clear perspective. It is against the postmodernist clarity of seeing traditions, rituals, and incontrovertible sacred texts as impediments to the global multi-cultural advancement occurring in an age of electronic technology. UMAC's recession to archaism, to anachronistic dogmatism, to recidivism, is a direct challenge to all states that envision a new era in world history with the advent of the new millennium. Self-conscious of its inadequacies in meeting the demands of global progress, it is negative in thought and claims divine transcendental inspiration in enforcing ideological absurdities and rigidities on unsuspecting citizens, grounding their inflexible theses on the premises of a divine text. Their doctrines are a manifestation of demonic tendencies that every secular state has to guard against, and their vision of martyrdom leading to the gates of Paradise a virulent narcotic that provides the adherents with the motive of engaging in terror, in jihad against postmodernist states that have left the threshold of medieval ecclesiasticism.

The Islamic amalgam of state and religion as one indivisible entity is in contestation with the enlightened democratic concept of the division between state and church, between secularism and religious ideology. This amalgam is pivotal to fundamentalism, and the cleavage is a threat to UMAC's hegemonic thrust to conquer, to secure for itself all-embracing power in the body politic. There can be no reconciliation by secularism with the militant Islamic ethos that seeks to cloud the expanding horizons of the new millennium.

There were various annexures to the report, giving the number of cells established throughout the city, the executive members of the cells, the number of meetings held, and the newspapers that supported UMAC.

Much discussion followed after the presentation of the report. Salman kept Mr Khamsin's advice in mind and said little, discreetly confining himself to agreeing with the views of other Ministers or making neutral statements such as:

'There is a crisis certainly.'

'We are faced with a serious problem but have the will to overcome it'.

'The youth are certainly vulnerable'.

The President commended the commission that had been established by the Minister of Safety and Security to examine the situation and present its findings. He concluded by saying that 'no effort would be spared to counter the fundamentalist revolutionaries at their very doorsteps by the might of the state.'

In the evening Salman gave Mr Khamsin the report to read. After he had read it he said he hoped that Salman had remained silent.

'I made a few non-committal statements and that was all.'

'I am afraid neutrality might not work if the situation worsens.'

'What shall we do?'

'We must wait. When there is turmoil in the state then emotion enters and reason evaporates. All Muslims will be branded as fundamentalists.'

'We must not allow that to happen.'

'We will have to decide on our loyalties. In the meantime, let us hope that the fire does not spread.'

When Salman returned home for the week-end he was troubled. Was the formation of UMAC the prelude to the eventual fulfillment of the third prophecy? That a penumbra was creeping over the land no one could deny. The prisons still contained many inmates. Commissions of inquiry into graft and corruption were being established in all the provinces; state services were declining in efficiency; professionals of all types were resigning and some emigrating; and the World Health Organisation had stated that Aids was spreading faster than in other countries on the continent. Johannesburg, once the great centre of commerce and wealth, was decaying. Derelict buildings were inhabited by unemployed workers and many thousands of migrants from sub-Saharan countries that were in a state of war, anarchy and poverty. The first prophecy had been fulfilled, and the second one was now assuming full reality.

The third prophecy was of an entirely different order, for it hung in a distant firmament. Was UMAC the organisation, though now part of the thickening penumbra, that would eventually bring forth the man of destiny ordained to restore civic order and tranquillity?

X

ONE FRIDAY MR KHAMSIN said to Salman: 'Come with me to the mosque today.'

'How can I? I would be a hypocrite.'

'Listen to me. Muslims have become militant in the city. They will not stop opposing the drug merchants and the criminals and also the administration if it does not act against them. You hold an important position in the Cabinet. Your attendance at mosque will be interpreted as moral support. For your own safety you cannot alienate them.'

'I have not entered a mosque for many years. Ismail, you are asking me to undertake an act that my intelligence ... '

'Intelligence? There are realities that demand compromise. To exist one must bend. There is a saying: "Trees that do not sway in the wind are soon uprooted".'

'I must speak to Elizabeth.'

'Listen, forget Elizabeth. We are in Cape Town, among Muslims who are opposing the administration.'

'What will others in parliament say when they see me in the mosque?'

'You have never proclaimed that you're an atheist.'

'That's true.'

'So what can they say? Come with me now.'

'Give me time till next Friday to consider.'

He agonised over his friend's request. He did not ask Elizabeth for her opinion. In the office he could not concentrate on his work. Allison inquired if he had a headache and if she could give him some Panado tablets.

'Yes, please.'

He ruminated on the second prophecy. The country was certainly in a dark phase and he was being sucked in by the events. Mr Roma was a visionary. There was no doubt. Could he refuse his friend's request to accompany him to the mosque?

When Friday came Mr Khamsin asked him again to accompany him. He hesitated.

'If the others in the assembly see me will they not be surprised and make derisory remarks?'

'There are many mosques. We shall go to one that is farthest away.'

He thought of Mr Bengali. Would he not look at him as a man to be despised. Or even come up to him in the presence of others and say that he was glad to see him realise the value of religion after years of disbelief.

'Please give me another week to decide.'

When he returned home he was on the verge, several times, of telling Elizabeth of Mr Khamsin's proposal, but his nerve failed him. She would either laugh at him or be outraged.

The following Friday when Mr Khamsin again asked him he agreed impulsively. When he entered the gate of the mosque he was surprised that no one took any notice of him. He performed his ablution beside Mr Khamsin and then entered the mosque with him and sat down on the carpet. He did not see Mr Bengali or anyone else who knew him. The imam's sermon related to an incident in the life of the Prophet Muhammad. When he was being pursued by the warriors of his Quraysh persecutors he found sanctuary in a cave in the wilderness near Mecca. When they arrived there they saw a nesting dove nearby and a spider's web across the entrance. Believing that the web would have been broken and the dove flown had the Prophet entered, they left.

'This incident,' the imam said, 'has a meaning for us in these trying times. Those who are steadfast in their faith will not be abandoned by Allah to immoral pagans and their defenders. Our persecutors will be scattered like thistles by the Omnipotent. Have faith and stand up to the corrupt as our Prophet did.'

After prayers several men came up to them as they walked through the courtyard, greeted them and went on their way.

'You see,' Mr Khamsin said as they entered the limousine in the street, 'how easy it has been.'

'Yes,' he said, starting the car, 'sometimes one sees ghosts when there are none.'

Mr Khamsin was pleased at the statement. He felt he had saved Salman from hell-fire in the afterlife. Salman the apostate had taken the first step towards redemption.

Salman felt not only elated, but elevated in spirit. The mosque's interior had been full of light as the arched windows were large; the Persian design of the carpets beautiful; the mihrab or niche where the imam stood facing Mecca, attractively tiled in turquoise. The crystal chandeliers, though unlit, added to the serene ambience. He tried to recall the last time he had entered a mosque. When he attended school he had to accompany his father on Fridays. When he attended university he went occasionally in the company of some students, but when he went to England he never saw the interior of a mosque. After nearly thirty five years he had prayed again.

XI

MADAM NOMSA, THE MINISTER of Health, was in an extremely angry mood with members of the official Opposition during question time in parliament. She was asked to provide information on the number of clinics in the country, how many were in operation, whether new ones had been built, whether there was adequate medicine for patients (a newspaper reporter had alleged that at some clinics doctors could only give advice on ailments but not dispense medicine), how many doctors were employed and how many had resigned.

'The members of the Opposition must stop asking me these childish questions. I am not a baby.'

She was correct in her last statement. She was a woman in a short-sleeved tight dress with fat extruding from every part of her body that was uncovered. Her neck and back were thick, her rear prominence a hillock. She looked formidable with shoulders a Sumo wrestler would have esteemed. She was a woman no man would wish to confront outside the assembly chamber as she displayed fierce determination in everything she did or said.

'Honourable Minister,' Mr Darnel said, 'these questions must be answered. You are responsible for giving us the information. This is part of parliamentary procedure and you are obligated to the citizens of this country as well.'

'Let me tell you this, Honourable Mr Darnel. I was not elected by the citizens but nominated to this post by my party and the President.'

'You cannot escape your responsibility to provide the information requested. I am reliably informed that some clinics are not functioning.'

'If that is so why ask me?'

'I wish to know officially from the Minister of Health the state of the clinics. Surely the provincial ministers have provided you with relevant information.'

'Don't talk nonsense!' she shouted. 'Why didn't you ask them for the information before coming here.'

'It is my privilege to question you and your obligation to answer.'

Madam Nomsa had received severe criticism in the press as hospital and clinic services had deteriorated and therefore did not take kindly to interrogation. She was in a permanent state of bad temper.

'I am doing my best to reduce the evil Apartheid legacy that deprived my people of medical services.'

Mr Darnel was not a man to be put off by her statement. He had heard about the past too often from members of the ruling party to be content with the explanation.

'I want to know from you, Honourable Minister, how many doctors have resigned? Newspapers report that many of those who have resigned are leaving the country.'

'Let them go. I will get others from Russia and India to replace them.'

'Minister, let me read a section of an article that appeared in the *Daily Chronicle*, written by a journalist after a visit to the Southern Cross Hospital:

"To visit this hospital is a painful experience. One sees long queues of patients in corridors, having arrived in the early morning. As there are insufficient beds to accommodate patients who are under treatment, some are lying on the floor. I was told that because of a lack of bed linen, patients have to bring their own from home. The nurses walk past, indifferent to their plight.

"Outpatients have to wait for many long hours before receiving treatment, and many more hours before obtaining medicine from the dispensary. Some have to go home without receiving attention and return the next day. Doctors have resigned because of the unacceptable conditions prevailing, and those who remain forced to work long hours. What has led to this state of affairs? An answer is desperately needed from the Health Ministry."

'Madam Nomsa, is this what you term reducing the evil of the Apartheid legacy?'

'That journalist is a racist.'

'He is not a white.'

'That is the work of a white journalist using a black name.'

'His photograph appears next to the article.'

'That means nothing. They can use anyone's photograph. I will take up this matter with the Fraud Commission.'

'You may do that.'

Salman rose to defend the Minister.

'Honourable Mr Darnel, I would like to remind you that just as one swallow does not make a summer, one bat does not make a witch's brew.'

'Don't call me a bat,' Madam Nomsa shouted.

'Madam Nomsa, I am not calling you a bat. I am drawing an analogy.'

'Analogy? You called me a bat.'

'Honourable Minister, I did not call you a bat.'

'You did. And you will regret it,' she said, pointing a threatening finger.

As Salman did not respond, Mr Darnel came to his assistance. 'Madam Nomsa, what Dr Khan meant as I understood it, was that I had given one example, and those conditions do not prevail at all hospitals.'

'Don't try to fool me. Members of the Opposition have never complimented me and you are now trying to compliment me. Whatever I do is wrong and that is what you and that man over there are saying.'

Salman looked contrite and said:

'Honourable Minister, Madam Nomsa, I regret that my words have inadvertently offended you. I apologise sincerely for my statement and withdraw it.'

'The next time beware of calling me a bat,' she said, glaring at him. Salman looked at her helplessly.

'This discussion is now closed,' the Speaker of Parliament said. 'We shall now proceed to the questions to be directed to the Minister of Transport.'

During the lunch interval Salman made certain that he sat far away from Madam Nomsa. Mr Khamsin advised him, 'Silence in the chamber, occasionally, is discretion.'

'I supported her.'

'An angry person will misinterpret even support as defamation. She is not a woman who realises the value of criticism.'

And then Salman saw her coming towards him.

She stood beside his chair and said: 'Stand up, Minister.'

Salman, though fearing that she might attack him, stood up. She embraced him and kissed him on his cheeks, drawing him towards her ample hot body.

Everyone laughed.

She released him and said, 'I love you. Don't forget that.'

She went back to her table. Tears flooded her eyes and she wiped them with both hands.

Some days later Salman considered whether Madam Nomsa had come to embrace him after she regretted her misinterpretation of his defence, or whether she had a romantic motive. The gypsy had said that he would marry a big brown woman. Would that be Madam Nomsa? She was certainly a formidable woman and could devise the fall of the President. There was also the prophecy that he would be king. Lady Macbeth led her husband to the throne. Would Madam Nomsa lead him to the presidency? Were the prophecies of the 'fortune queens' statements of inevitable events to come? Could he alter what had been determined for him?

XII

ONE LATE AFTERNOON Salman and Mr Khamsin were sitting in the dining room of the Diaz Hotel. It was time for tea. The waiter came up to them. He first put the tray of cups, sugar bowl and teapot on the table and then placed an envelope before Salman. Without saying a word he walked away quickly.

Salman did not pick up the envelope. Its sudden appearance before him in a hotel dining room made him doubt its reality and for a moment he felt uncertain of his own existence. The envelope did not vanish and reality reasserted itself.

He saw that his name was not on it. He hesitated to touch it. The words 'letter bomb' flashed through his mind and fear filled him.

'It is for you.'

'My name's not on it.'

'Do you want me to open it?'

'I will open it.'

He did not want his friend to think he lacked courage. He opened the envelope and read the letter within:

'Dear Dr Salman Khan, as a senior Minister in the Cabinet of the government, I wish to speak to you on a matter of importance. I request your presence tomorrow night in the Chapel Street Mosque in the former District Six. – Yours in Islam, Saleem Anwar Sayid, President of UMAC.'

He handed the letter to Mr Khamsin, who said after reading it:

'I think you should go and meet the Shaykh. He is a learned man.'

'You will accompany me?'

'A third person will complicate matters.'

'Why do you think he wants to speak to me?'

'You know the state has branded UMAC as consisting of 'fundamentalists' and 'terrorists'. Some of them have been arrested. Perhaps he needs your help.'

'The organisation is under surveillance. I can be implicated.'

'I think he will be careful enough if he needs you. If I were you I would go.'

'There may be an informer in the mosque.'

'Do you remember that when I was appointed I wanted to see District Six? We drove through it and saw the mosque, the only building there. The Apartheid authorities never destroyed mosques in the suburbs they demolished. They feared the wrath of God. The Shaykh has decided to meet you there. I am sure you will be safe.'

Salman did not sleep well that night. At times fear surged through him. and he drank several glasses of water to calm himself. He was now not only a witness to the 'dark phase' in the country's history, but was being drawn into the thick of it. If his association with a conspiratorial organisation came to be known, he was doomed. The Intelligence Agency would waste no time in exposing him. The President would dismiss him from his post and he would be arraigned and condemned as a traitor. What should he do? Should he telephone Elizabeth in the morning and seek her advice? Should he cancel the meeting, plead prior commitments? He sat up on his bed, then went to the bathroom and washed his face with cold water and let it drip. He lay down, slept for a short while, woke with a start after he saw Macbeth in a dream, standing beside his bed, and uttering the words:

> Better be with the dead
> Whom we, to gain our peace, have sent to peace,
> Than on the torture of the mind to lie
> In restless ecstasy.

The next day Allison sensed that Salman was deeply troubled. She asked him if he was feeling unwell. He requested some Panado tablets and water.

'Thanks very much, Allison. These are trying times.'

'We have to stand up to them.'

'Yes, we have to.'

In the evening when the time for prayers neared he was extremely agitated and Mr Khamsin had to calm him.

'You must go for the sake of all Muslims in parliament. I can assure you that you will come to no harm. Shaykh Sayid is a well-respected theologian noted for his devotion to Islamic principles. He will take every precaution to protect you.'

He decided to go as he felt that his agony would be prolonged if he delayed.

Mr Khamsin said to him in the street before he entered his car:

'Do not accept any proposals that you think may compromise you. Tell the Shaykh you will consider.'

He parked the car opposite the mosque. No one came to meet him. Perhaps the Shaykh had decided to cancel the meeting. He sat for a while. When he heard the muezzin's prayer-call he alighted. In the mosque there were only about twenty worshippers. When prayers were over he remained seated. Everyone left besides a man who came towards him. He was tall, erect and dignified in bearing, with a bronze complexion, an aquiline nose, and a groomed pointed sorrel beard.

'Brother Salman, let us go into the room at the back.'

A tremor passed through him.

'We can sit here,' he proposed.

He felt that the mosque's interior would give him protection.

'Even mosque walls have ears.'

He followed. They went into a room at the back.

There were four women seated beside a table. They wore scarves over their heads. They stood up and salaamed. Shaykh Sayid gave Salman a chair and he sat down facing the women.

'Brother Salman, let me introduce you to the four ladies. They are Khatija, Ayesha, Maimuna and Hafsa. Do the names remind you of other names?'

56

He looked at their faces and remained silent.

'Four of the wives of our Prophet had the same names. Salman Rushdie defamed them in his novel *The Satanic Verses*. Do you remember?'

During the controversy in England over the novel, he had bought a copy, could not appreciate its modernist eclectic style, and had not read beyond fifty pages.

'Brother Salman, you are aware of the struggle of our ancestors here in the Cape for freedom from the Dutch colonialists in the seventeenth century. I am sure you have visited the shrine in Faure of Shaykh Yusuf who was exiled from Macassar?'

He did not answer.

That history, when he attended school, was not taught to him.

'The ladies here are the wives of prisoners held in Victory Prison. They are the mothers of twelve children.'

He looked at them and had the illusion of seeing a quartet of identical faces staring at him.

'Brother Salman, you know their husbands have been jailed for six years for possessing unlicensed firearms. They are in a dormitory of criminals we have decided to eliminate from society as the government has not only failed, but gives them protection. You, as a Muslim, will appreciate that for the husbands of these ladies to be in the company of those who drink and take drugs is abhorrent. There is also the danger they may be killed.'

'Shaykh Sayid, I am not responsible for their imprisonment.'

'Of course not. You would not imprison Muslim brothers among immoral people. Can you have them placed in a separate cell, and allow them to receive home food?'

'Shaykh Sayid, the prisons are overcrowded.'

'Yes, we knew that would happen when the death sentence was abolished. If you help the four husbands of these wives they will be grateful.'

'I will visit the prison and speak to the superintendent,' Salman conceded, eager to leave.

'Allah be praised. You will earn His blessings.'

Salman stood up, but the Shaykh restrained him.

'Sit for a while. Look.'

There was a cloth coverlet on the middle of the table. He removed it and Salman saw a large white envelope.

'Take it and open it.'

Salman thought of a letter bomb again and hesitated.

Saleem Sayid took the envelope, opened the flap and extracted a document which he handed to Salman, whose vision became blurred for a moment, then cleared.

'Do you recognise the document?'

He did not answer. What he had in his hand was a photocopy of the document on UMAC presented at the Cabinet meeting. For an instant his perception of where he was faded. He was in the boardroom of the President's chamber, the document before him.

'You have surely seen it before.'

The illusion vanished.

'Yes.'

'When it was read at Cabinet level did anyone question the truth of the allegations?'

'No.' He wanted to inquire how a copy of a confidential document could have reached his organisation, but could not.

'I know what you are thinking, brother Salman. How did this document come into my hands? That I cannot tell you now, but one day I shall, if Allah wills.'

Then the Shaykh asked one of the women to read an extract from the Qur'an. When she had finished, he inquired:

'Brother Salman, do you understand classical Arabic?'

'No,' he answered, feeling diminished.

'I will translate the verses for you:'

> "Have you seen him who denies our religion?
> It is he who harshly repels the orphan
> and does not urge others to feed the needy.

58

Woe to those who pray
but are heedless of their prayers;
who put on a show of piety
but refuse to give even the smallest help to others".'

There was silence for a moment. Then the Shaykh said:

'Brother Salman, we have taken every precaution to see that no one will know of your visit. We will remain here while you go to your car. You will see two men in the street near your car. They will walk away when you approach. Our best salaams to you and may Allah protect you.'

He walked out, saw the two men, got into his car and drove away. When he entered the hotel lounge Mr Khamsin was waiting for him. He was in familiar surroundings again, felt relieved and related his meeting with the Shaykh and the request made.

'You will have to help them. Do you know the superintendent of Victory Prison?'

'Yes, I have spoken to him and inspected the prison.'

'Who is he?'

'A Mr Reed.'

'Was he there before transition?'

'Yes.'

'Do not go to him.'

'Should I call him to my office?'

'No. Meet him at the Sea View Restaurant. We have been there. Speak to him after lunch about what he must do.'

'You think of everything, Ismail.'

'Tell him that the four men need privacy to pray as they are devout Muslims. They recite the Qur'an every day and prefer home food. Tell him that the previous government respected the Muslim religion. They did not destroy mosques. Suggest that he will be rewarded some time in the future, but be careful. A word. A hint.'

Salman met Mr Reed at the Sea View Restaurant and after lunch had no difficulty in making him agree to grant the privileges he requested for the four men.

'Thanks very much, Mr Reed. You know very well that criminals who carry AKs and kill are seldom arrested.'

'Don't tell me what I know, Minister. I go through hell looking after petty criminals when the big ones get away with millions from the banks. In the past they never got away. Our friends in prison never used the weapons they carried.'

'Friends, that's a very accurate description. I shall remember your appreciation of the situation and the families of our friends will bless you.'

After a week another letter was delivered to Salman by the same waiter in the same way as before. He opened it and read:

'There will surely come a time when Truth shall prevail and the forces of evil in rebellion against the Omnipotent, dispersed. Your assistance is appreciated and you will receive the favour and grace of Allah.'

After Mr Khamsin read the letter, he commented:

'The episode has ended happily for you. You can imagine what could have happened if you had denied them help. The curses of hundreds, perhaps thousands.'

Salman did not tell Mr Khamsin that he had been shown the report on UMAC. He felt that if he did he would break an implicit covenant between him and Saleem Sayid and that could lead to retribution.

That night, after switching off the bedside lamp, he felt a profound sense of contentment. He had conferred ease on four prisoners and given their wives the satisfaction of providing home food for their husbands.

XIII

ON A SUNDAY MR KHAMSIN telephoned Salman. 'Come with me to the Mayfair Mosque today for midday prayers. Afterwards you and Elizabeth will have lunch with my family.'

'What will she say when she comes to hear?'

'We are not asking her to convert.'

Salman and Elizabeth went to Mr Khamsin's residence. His mansion was one of the largest in the suburb. Elizabeth enjoyed visiting Mr Khamsin's three wives and their thirteen children. They were always happy to see her and talk to her of domestic affairs.

When the time came for prayers Mr Khamsin said: 'Salman, come with me. Some day Elizabeth will know that you attend Friday prayers in Cape Town. You might as well let her know now. I will inform her in front of my wives that you are coming with me to the mosque. When you go home you can explain to her, but your act will have been done.'

He agreed reluctantly.

Mr Khamsin went to the kitchen where his wives and daughters were preparing lunch. Elizabeth was making salad. He said to her, 'Elizabeth, I am now going to the mosque for prayers. Salman is accompanying me. I hope you don't mind.'

'Take him if he wishes to go with you.'

She did not show any surprise. She was busy shredding lettuce leaves.

He returned to Salman in the lounge.

'You don't know much about women,' he said. 'I have three wives. Elizabeth was not upset when I told her. The salad she was preparing was more important to her.'

Salman, sitting in Mr Khamsin's black Daimler Sovereign on the way to the mosque, felt relaxed. Having attended mosque in Cape Town, he experienced no difficulty in entering the gate of the Mayfair mosque. Again the worshippers, intent on their devotions, seemed oblivious of his presence. After prayers, in the courtyard, several men approached Mr Khamsin, greeted him and Salman. One man, in a green robe and turban, invited them to his home for lunch. Mr Khamsin declined by telling him, 'My three wives will divorce me and where shall I find three others in these times.'

'There are many in parliament,' the man replied.

Mr Khamsin relished the reply, but Salman did not. He regarded the man's reply as a snide attack on the dignity of parliamentary representatives.

On the way home, Mr Khamsin said to him in the car, 'We cannot be serious at all times. If we do not have a sense of humour, we may not remain afloat in the sea of life.'

Salman enjoyed lunch with Mr Khamsin's family. There was an array of platters: starters of prawn and lobster garnished with spiced mushroom sauce, fish laden with crushed garlic and butter, marinated lamb, chicken and steak, home-baked naan, salads of many varieties and desserts laden with pistachio nuts, blanched almond slices, cherries, kiwi fruit and pears in cinnamon syrup.

Later, Mr Khamsin and Salman went to the lounge. Two maids brought spiced coffee and dainties.

'Everyone in your family is very happy,' Salman said, recalling the joy on the faces of his wives and children during lunch.

'There is much truth in the saying, "the more the merrier". Our religion meets every contingency. If you had not abandoned Islam you could have married another woman or two and have had children.'

'Elizabeth would never have accepted a rival.'

'You lack experience with women. Always make proposals at the right moment and you will succeed. And often the right moment is when they are engaged in the kitchen preparing food. See how I got Elizabeth to agree.'

'I wonder what I would have done without your help. Probably resigned from my post and left for England.'

When the women came into the lounge Mr Khamsin proposed that they should all go to the Zoo Lake in Parkview. They would have late afternoon tea there and the children would play games on the lawns. They agreed. Mr Khamsin and Salman went in the Daimler while the wives and children followed in other cars.

When they reached the lake the two men sat on a bench near the edge and looked at the waterfowl and swans floating by.

'Do you know, Salman, that your name is the same as that of a famous disciple of the Prophet Muhammad?'

'No. Who was he?'

'Salman, the Persian. That is why you had to become a believer again.'

He did not comment on that statement. He had merely conceded to perform the compulsory ritual within mosque precincts to please his friend.

'I must make a study of Islamic history. I have been negligent, concentrating on European history.'

'I must introduce you to a mufti. He will teach you.'

'Do you remember the third prophecy of Mr Roma during the television discussion before the second election?'

'Yes. He said that one day a Muslim would rule this country.'

'Do you think that is possible?'

'That was a prophecy and anything is possible. There is nothing fixed in this world though theorists would have us believe so. One man can do more than thousands in parliament. He may be the mahdi.'

'You speak of a man. In parliament we have over a hundred women.'

'No wonder things are going wrong. They should be in kitchens.'

'A mahdi, you said. Someone like a messiah.'

'Yes, a man of wisdom.'

'The prophecy is strange … very strange.'

Three children came running towards them and said that tea was ready. They went towards a clump of trees where the wives were seated.

That evening when Salman and Elizabeth returned home, she did not comment on his visit to the mosque. He was perplexed. Why did she not comment on the betrayal of his secular principles? Was there an occult power determining her mind to the acceptance of spiritual realities? Was this a stage in the fulfillment of the third prophecy, that he would be the man to transform the country from its present declining state to civic order and economic resurgence?

That night, in bed, he read the Sunday newspapers and when his wife fell asleep he looked at her. He thought of what Mr Khamsin had told him of the Islamic privilege of marriage to other women. His love life with Elizabeth had become stale. The few early years of intimacy had passed swiftly and both of them had never expressed the desire to have children. Nor did they arrive.

They had applied themselves to their careers – Elizabeth had worked as a secretary to a firm of accountants and devoted herself to the Socialist Party's efforts to secure liberation in South Africa. How fortunate Mr Khamsin was. Three wives! What enjoyment!

If he had remained a Muslim he too could have had three wives. The welfare of his children would have kept him out of the mire of obsession with his own self embroiled in official work that brought no joy to him. He fell asleep for a few hours and woke after a dream in which he saw children playing with a ball on a stretch of lawn beside the lake and laughing joyfully as it fell into the water.

XIV

WHEN SALMAN, THE NEXT DAY, returned to his office in Cape Town he looked at Allison. She was a woman of about forty years, very efficient, pleasant, with a ripe figure. His relationship with her had always been strictly professional. He had never asked her any personal questions. She came to work in the morning, carried out her duties efficiently, arranged for tea and refreshments when meetings were held in the boardroom, made appointments, and delivered instructions to subordinate officials in other rooms. He had not faulted her, and at all times displayed respect and courtesy. She had been very considerate when he was troubled and offered him Panado tablets, but now decided that it was time he knew her better.

'Allison,' he said, when she came into the office with a document to be signed, 'may I ask you a personal question?'

She was surprised. Then she smiled and said, 'Why not?'

'Thank you. Tell me, were you ever married?'

'Yes, for eleven months exactly.'

'That was a brief relationship.'

'Some men are impossible to live with.'

'And some women too.'

'I hope I am not impossible to work with.'

'On the contrary, Allison, I don't know what I would do without you. Please sit down.' She sat down on the arm of a chair near the door. She wore a charcoal skirt, a pink blouse, and her fleshy legs were very smooth.

'You know, Allison, I have never said a kind word to you.'

'Nor an angry one,' she smiled.

'Nor asked you about your private life.'

'You have been very negligent.'

He liked her response.

'Well, I don't want to be accused of negligence any longer. Will you join me for lunch this afternoon?'

'In the dining-hall?'

'We shall go to a restaurant.'

'You have an appointment with Mr Winter at two and we may not be back by then.'

'Cancel the appointment.'

They went to the Sea View Restaurant. After lunch he proposed:

'Allison, this coming Saturday I will not be going home for the weekend. Can we meet?'

'Why not?'

'Where?'

'Come to my apartment.'

'That's a date,' he said, elated.

On Friday he told Mr Khamsin that he would not be flying back home with him as he had much pressing work to complete before Monday. He had already telephoned Elizabeth.

He felt very excited in the evening and when night came he lay awake in bed with a sense of contentment. All the stresses he had undergone faded from memory. Miss Allison's ripe figure filled his consciousness with the certainty of romance. A second wife! Now Mr Khamsin would not be the only one to enjoy more than one woman.

The next day he drove to Allison's apartment building. When she opened the door he saw a transformed woman: she wore a flowing light blue dress, and her brown hair had been let down. She did not resemble the woman he knew during office hours. She was now wearing stiletto-heeled shoes so that she was taller than him. He had expected to find her in a transparent nightdress, ready for love.

'Let us go for a drive along the coast first,' she said, 'and later have lunch. Afterwards we can decide how to spend the afternoon.'

He suppressed his disappointment. She put on a straw hat that added to her gay appearance and they left the apartment.

Later, after the drive, he said to her as they sat down at a table under the awning-covered terrace of the Sea View Restaurant:

'I am putting myself in your care and will have whatever you select for me on the menu.'

'You want to be under my care?'

'With pleasure and very willingly.'

'I treat my slaves very badly.'

'I promise not to rebel.'

He enjoyed Allison's company. This was the first time in his conjugal life that he was alone with another woman who evoked within him a strong romantic sentiment. He had spent the night in desire for her and here she was on a beautiful day with the sea before them.

He relished the food she selected and when they had finished she suggested that they go to the cableway station and go up Table Mountain.

'Why there and not elsewhere?'

He wished to go to her apartment.

'So that we can be above Parliament Building.'

'Why above?'

'It is not a place of pleasure, is it?'

'You always have the right answer.'

They walked towards the car and Salman opened the door for her. He drove to the cableway station and soon they reached the top of the mountain. Salman felt he had ascended a stage towards heaven.

'This is the first time I have come up here,' he confessed.

'Why the delay?'

'Perhaps because the mountain is so close to the city. One always seeks adventure in distant places.'

She stopped walking, looked at him and smiled.

'You want to be adventurous today? Why not? Put your arm around my waist.'

He obliged.

'You are so different from Allison, my secretary,' he said as a sense of exhilaration gripped him.

'You are not a Minister now. You are my willing slave and must do what you are told.'

'Yes madam.'

They walked for an hour, looked at the plants that were different from those below and, when they stood near the edge, saw the vastness of the Atlantic Ocean.

'I am in paradise,' he whispered.

'This paradise is above. Do you know the paradise below?'
'Below? Where?'

'Below.'

'But where?'

'Where there is sin.'

'Sin?'

'Have you read the Bible?'

'Some of it. Many years ago.'

'I read it regularly. It says that the earthly paradise is the sweetest.'

'I didn't know my secretary was interested in riddles.'

'When we go down the riddle will be solved.'

'Look at the ocean Allison, the sky, the lovely clouds. How can paradise be below.'

'You have not been initiated,' she said, placing her hand on his shoulder. 'You must kiss me now.'

He hesitated. 'I order you.'

He obliged her lightly on her cheek. 'Again.'

He obliged her, but this time she turned and embraced him. Releasing him she said, 'You still don't understand that the real paradise is below.'

'Below the mountain?'

'No. Further down.'

'You must teach me.'

'I will. Even Adam learnt nothing above.'

XV

AFTER HAVING ENJOYED ALLISON'S warm embrace in her apartment, Salman felt that his devotion to politics had disengaged him from sensual pleasures. In fact, at home, he was often an ascetic for several weeks at a time for Elizabeth's devotion to Marxist ideology did not extend to the marriage bed. The time had come to enjoy himself sensually and forget his responsibilities. The enjoyment of women would be the antidote to the daily indignity of his existence. Every time he went to the airport or returned home, he would look at the caravans and think of the three 'fortune queens'. He decided that he would visit them and enjoy one every week. A sense of pleasure coursed through him. With Allison and the gypsies he would have four women in his harem, one more than his friend, or two more if he included Elizabeth.

On a Saturday afternoon he went to visit the gypsies. Again as on the first occasion he knocked on the door of the caravan, no one answered, and he was returning to his car in disappointment, when the door opened and he heard the words he had heard on his first visit:

'Don't go way, sir, we here.'

He smiled happily and went towards her. They entered the caravan. He was pleased to see the other two sisters seated at the table strewn with cards. He greeted them and sat down, delighted to be with his gypsy harem.

'You want to know more fortune?'

'No, I want to enjoy you.'

'Injoy?'

'You today.'

'No fortune, but injoy?'

The queens laughed and clapped their hands.

'You pay to injoy.'

'How much?'

'Too much. We better than wife. Your wife wood.'

'How did you know that?'

'Fortune queens know everything.'

They laughed and he laughed with them.

'You pay one thousand five hundred and injoy we three.'

'I enjoy one every week,' he responded, his sensuality aroused by her erotic pronunciation of the verb.

'No. Three queens today. Then you man.'

This was a demand he could not consummate. They were wild exotic females of primitive lust.

'Please, I enjoy one today, one next week. I make you wives and look after you.'

'No. You injoy we three and pay. Or you not leave caravan.'

She stood up, looking like an angry empress.

'Please, only one today.'

The other women stood up and said in a chorus, 'You injoy we three.'

Salman became apprehensive. They were lustful women and were determined to have their way. Could he retreat unscathed? He stood up.

The 'empress' came round the table and embraced him. Her two sisters moved towards him, held him, and turned him round and round and sang, 'Injoy, injoy.' He felt dazed. 'You injoy we three or pay.'

'I pay.'

He was alone with three maenads. Desire drained out of him. He had come to make them his concubines and now found them dictating to him.

He took out his purse and gave over the one thousand rands it contained.

'More!'

He shook the purse.

She counted the money.

'Next week bring five hundred or we curse.'

The three women joined hands, danced round him and sang, 'Curse! Curse!' Their bangles chimed and he felt he was a prisoner in Aladdin's cave.

When they stopped he was told by the 'empress': 'You bring money next week and we give good fortune.'

'Yes.'

'You promise?'

'Yes.'

She opened the door and he went out into a sunlit world. He stood for a while to regain his bearings and then walked towards his car. Another car drove in and three men emerged. He saw that they were gypsies. They were sunburnt men with elegant moustaches that film actors of the forties liked. They came towards him. The 'queens' came out of the caravan and stood nearby.

'Why you look worried? You not get good fortune?' the tallest man of the three inquired.

Salman forced a smile.

'He getting lots money next week,' the empress said.' He promise bring five hundred.'

'Good, good. We come from Romania. You know where?'

'Yes.'

'You must visit Romania. Very good place. You go home safe now,'

He entered his car and drove away. The 'queens' did not blow kisses at him this time.

XVI

As THE YEAR WORE OUT and the new year began the third prophecy reasserted itself in Salman's consciousness. He had to establish who would be the man to rule the country as his future depended on that knowledge. He was convinced that the third prophecy would attain fulfilment as the first one had swiftly come to fruition, and the second one had been frighteningly manifested by Madam Nomsa's display of irrationality and in his own descent into a world where he was 'cabin'd, cribb'd, confined' and a 'walking shadow'. Perhaps Saleem Anwar Sayid was the man who would be selected by destiny to rule. He had the personality, wisdom and courage. But his organisation was based in the Cape and did not enjoy the support of Muslims in the rest of the country. Besides, the state's security forces were pitted against 'fundamentalists' and 'terrorists' and his organisation would not be able to escape destruction. And certainly not that viper, Mr Bengali, who never missed a day in parliament nor articulated a word. Besides, he was under Intelligence surveillance and his appearance excluded him.

The days and months passed. Then it occurred to Salman that the man whose credentials suggested a future President was Shareef Suhail. In parliament he had been an admired and respected figure. He was the only man who had resigned and though he had offered no reason other than 'private and personal considerations', his absence had always been felt. He was an orator with an arresting voice and an excellent command of the English language. In Apartheid times he had been imprisoned on Dragon Island for his political writing and after transition nominated by the African Front as a parliamentary representative. He had not been afraid to criticise the party when necessary. He was a historian of repute with published work on imperialist expansion in the East, and comparative studies of Western and Eastern philosophy, an essayist and literary critic.

He had dominated parliament with his presence. There had been much speculation in the press when he resigned. Some newspaper editors said that he had perceived that the administration was moving in the direction of totalitarianism, clearly evident in the monolithic party structure that rejected opposition, or criticism and even descended to defamatory remarks.

While Shareef Suhail was in parliament he had spoken to him many times but had not cultivated his friendship. He had much to do to dismantle the edifice of privileged white education. Could he now approach him and speak to him without arousing suspicion of some secret motive? And what would he say to him? The obsession to discover the next ruler of the country drove him on and he decided to pay him a social visit. He knew that he lived in Fordsburg. He scanned the Johannesburg telephone directory, found his telephone number, and asked Allison to make an appointment for him on a Saturday afternoon.

He drove to Shareef Suhail's apartment building situated close to the Oriental Plaza, a hive of shops built during the Apartheid era after the inhabitants of the central section of the suburb had been forcibly removed and banished to the distant township of Lenasia, south of the city. When he knocked at the door of the apartment Shareef appeared and said cordially, 'Come in Salman. I am very pleased to see you again.'

They sat down in the lounge.

In parliament Shareef had always looked very distinguished, in a black, dark blue or green Arabian mantle. He was now dressed in a flowing pearl-white shirt with an open neck that displayed his muscular torso, and grey pants. His face was clean shaven; in parliament he had a neatly trimmed beard. His appearance surprised and unsettled Salman for a moment as he had visualised him looking as he had known him two years before.

'Have you come to see me on some important matter?'

Shareef had observed the bewilderment on his visitor's face.

'O, nothing important.'

In his eagerness to see the man who could be the next president he had not given attention to what he would say to him.

'I have not seen you for some time and decided to visit you.'

'That is a good reason. How are you getting on in your portfolio?'

'Not well. You know the Education portfolio was taken away from me after the second election.'

'Were you given a reason?'

'No. The President wanted to humiliate me.'

'He respected you. That was the impression I had.'

'Yes, before the election. He did not want me to rise higher.'

'Rise higher?'

'As Vice-President.'

'He kept you on, though giving you another portfolio. He dropped others.'

'He kept me on as he did not wish to create the impression he was against all those who were out of the country.'

'He too was in exile.'

'I am sure after the next election I will be axed.'

'The next election will be constituency-based. The political scene will change radically. You could be the next president.'

'You really think so?'

'The world of politics is not governed by the laws of physics. You should know that.'

'Yes, the African Front can be defeated.'

Shareef stood up and said that he would get some apple juice. He went to the kitchen and returned with two glasses on a tray and a decanter of juice. He handed Salman a glass.

'Thank you,' Salman whispered, feeling diminished in the presence of the tall, well-built man.

'Do you exercise?' he asked.

'I go to the gymnasium several times a week.'

'I wish I could do that. These days I feel like a prisoner,' he confessed.

'If you feel that way why not resign?'

'What reason could I give?'

'I gave no reason.'

'You must have had.'

'I did not have to make it public.'

'You do not wish to return to politics?'

'I am quite happy reading, writing and reflecting.'

'I have to go now. Thanks for the hospitality.'

'You must come again.'

He went home and brooded. Shareef Suhail was a man in superb control of himself, intelligent, handsome, a man whose physical and mental gifts functioned in harmony. He was not racked by the kind of undignified work he was involved in, which left lacerations within. He had no ambition to be the head of the state, nor regretted abandoning his parliamentary seat and salary. The third prophecy could not refer to him. His preference was for the life of a scholar.

Why could he not be like him; have the courage to resign and lead a tranquil existence, devoting himself to studies? He had sufficient funds in the bank to maintain himself and Elizabeth to the end of their days. Did his professorship at Cambridge and his presidency of the Socialist Party condemn him to his present ignominious position? He was a slave, controlled by the head of the state, answerable to him and the public for whatever he did, a pawn on the checkerboard of politics. For the next three years he would remain a serf. If only he knew who would be the next president he would be at ease. He could then decide on his future. Mr Khamsin had mentioned that his first name was the same as that of one of the famous disciples of the Prophet Muhammad. Did that portend anything? As for his surname, there were others. Genghis Khan. Kubla Khan. They were famous kings. Empire builders. Conquerors. Renowned for all time in world history. Was he a descendant? His name must have some connection with those royal personages. Both emperors had hundreds of wives and concubines and perhaps one of their male descendants was his ancestor. His name pleased him. He was certainly the man who would achieve fame. The third prophecy referred to him, he had attended mosque and was now a believer. Mr Khamsin was right. God works in ways that mortals with finite intelligence cannot fathom.

An idea came to him. He hurried to his study, opened the Oxford Dictionary and searched for the word 'khan':

Title of rulers and officials in Central Asia, Afghanistan, (Hist.) supreme ruler of Turkish, Tartar and Mongol tribes, and emperor of China, in Middle Ages. (From Turki kān lord)

Happiness suffused him. He was certainly a descendant of the famous line of noblemen, conquerors, emperors. Then he saw the word above 'khamsin': Oppressive hot S or SE wind in Egypt for about 50 days in March, April and May. (Arab 'kamsün' fifty)

The irony of his friend's name struck him. He was not a man of closed nature, but a vivacious man. He later told him of the lexical entries.

'Congratulations. There is no doubt that you are a descendant of the great khans. Kismet is going to make you famous. As for me I am of Arabian blood. Therefore I have three wives.'

Salman enjoyed the comment. He thought of his conquest, Allison, his concubine. And he may yet be able to conquer the three 'fortune queens'. Kismet.

'Who knows. Present adversity may lead to triumph in time to come. You may be the man of the hour.'

Salman was deeply conscious of his reliance on his friend. He had sustained him when he was demoted from the Education portfolio, taken him to mosque, restored his faith, and advised him how to deal with Saleem Anwar Sayid. His statement was a clear reference to the third prophecy, to its inevitable realisation.

XVII

SHAREEF SUHAIL, A MONTH after Salman's visit, received the following letter from the former President:

'Now that I am alone in my home in Orange Grove Park in East London, I have often thought of the time when we – those in exile and those under lock and key on Dragon Island, as you were – lost all hope that we would one day return in triumph to our homeland. And when that happened it was beyond our expectation. The oppressors surrendered. The entire country, with all its gold and diamonds, was handed over to us on a platter. That had never happened in history before.

'Rulers are never willing to give up power and wealth. You are a historian. You know.

'You and many comrades were imprisoned on Dragon Island. There you were all forced to build the great stone citadel that now stands as a monument to your defiance of the oppressors. Many died in its construction. It will stand there for centuries to come. When I went there three months ago in the company of several diplomats from Tibet, I was surprised to see that the commemorative board at the portal, on which the names of all comrades had been inscribed in gold lettering, had been removed. I took the liberty of questioning the governor of the Island, and he informed me that the order had come from 'higher authority'. He went on to say, rather insolently and in front of the diplomats, that who was I to question the order. This has always been the fate of those who sacrifice themselves for the sake of liberty. They are soon forgotten.

'In Russia the statues of Marx, Lenin and Tolstoy no longer stand on pedestals. They have been overturned, smashed and taken away in trucks. The pieces now lie in a deep ravine. I am informed that the statue of Michael Kava and other singers now stand on the pedestals and that tourists come from all over the world to worship them with uplifted arms. You have seen these worshippers on television screens when singers arrive in our country. They jump and scream like demented barbarians on stages erected in stadia.

'I shall, before you and all the other valiant comrades are forgotten, write to President Zara and tell him to have your names engraved on granite like that of the pharaohs and placed at the entrance of the citadel. I will also request him to inscribe the following warning below: "Whoever desecrates these hallowed names shall die of AIDS."

'The new dispensation was a challenge to us. Your presence in parliament was always valued by me. I felt that all those who struggled with us were single-minded in the conviction that we would not imitate the actions of our former oppressors and would govern the country with absolute integrity. Then you resigned. I did not question you as your brief statement suggested some turmoil involving a woman had overtaken you (I have, fortunately, kept away from women all my life).

'Now that we are both outside the political corral, you will perhaps tell me what led to your decision.

'I am now a recluse. The only visitors I have are tourists. No one in this country is interested in me.

'I read a story by an Egyptian writer in a magazine a few days ago. As it is in hieroglyphs I have translated it for you. It is a fantasy.'

THE HAWK

There was once an Egyptian hawk that wished to make a complaint to the League of Civilised States. When this organisation held a meeting in the city of Alexandria, it flew into one of the open windows of the domed hall where the delegates were seated and took its perch on the lectern. At this moment the President, a frail old man with a scowling face – his appearance the antithesis of pharaohs such as Akhenaton and Rameses II- entered the hall with ten bodyguards. He sat down in the front row of seats facing the hawk, and his bodyguards positioned themselves, five on either side of the stage. The hawk addressed the League members:

'Mr President and members of this august assembly, I have come to make a serious complaint. But before that, I find it strange that there are only men here representing the nations of the world. Are there no women with the beauty and intelligence of Queen Cleopatra in your domains? Do women not constitute half the human species on earth?

'Now to the heart of my complaint. I wish to place on record in this assembly a strong objection to the term "hawk" used in every country in the world to describe men or states that are aggressive and war-like. I cannot understand why the word has found its way into your vocabularies. We hawks follow nature in our lives. Nature has ordained that we should eat rodents and other creatures that might endanger its equilibrium. We do not kill because we are vicious or sadistic. In one of your holy texts it is written that the Divinity says: "We have created everything by measure." Now this applies to the realm of nature from which the human race has excluded itself by using the gift of intelligence to devise weapons of death and destruction. You will appreciate that the term "hawk" applied deprecatingly to human beings slanders us in that we act according to the Creator's primordial design while you act against it. Some of your philosophers have actually come to the conclusion that life is absurd and revolt and annihilation the only options; you may say that you use the word metaphorically. Nevertheless, the analogy's slanderous as it purports to embrace our natures. I advise you not to use … '

At this moment the President rose from his seat, with some difficulty because of his spindly legs, lifted his two shaking hands and pointing at the five guards on either side of the stage, croaked: 'Kill that wild bird!'

The hawk had already intuitively sensed what was to happen. It left its perch with a sudden upward flight as the guards fired their guns. The bullets sped across the stage and struck each of them. They fell down dead.

The hawk saw this from above and returning to its perch on the lectern went on to say:

'August representatives, you have now witnessed a demonstration of your perverse natures. I plead with you not to use my name again to describe your violent dispositions.'

The hawk rose, flew over the President's head – he shielded himself with his hands in fear – then circled over the heads of the terrified representatives of the civilised states of the world, finally sailing out of one of the windows in the dome of the assembly hall.

Shareef Suhail wrote the following reply:

'I received your letter and the enclosed fantasy which I found very interesting. You say that the shattered statues of Marx, Lenin and Tolstoy are now lying somewhere in a ravine. The pieces may yet be retrieved and reassembled some day, ages hence, by archaeologists and placed in a museum.

'As for the citadel, I have to inform you, regretfully, that after your visit, it was deconstructed stone by stone by the order of a 'higher authority'. The stones were taken away by a cargo vessel and now lie fathoms deep in the Pacific Ocean. The citadel will never rise again as the vessel, on its return journey, was caught in a typhoon and destroyed. Sadly, the captain and his crew perished so that no one will ever know where the stones lie on the ocean floor.

'You inquire why I resigned. The answer partly resided in 'domestic turmoil' (your insight is uncannily accurate) and partly in the views presented in an article I wrote for a journal entitled *Perceptions*. I enclose a photocopy herewith.'

The following is the text of Shareef Suhail's article:

DEMOCRACY : DOES IT EXIST?

The existence of democracy in a modern state is a myth. The term means rule by the authority of the people, derived from the Greek root words *demos*, people, and *kratia*, power. In the sixth century BC it was a political system introduced by Solon in the city-state of Athens permitting all males to participate in the civic assembly and take administrative decisions. In modern times, because of population density and other factors, it refers to the practice of electing from several rival political parties representatives to Parliament or Congress. This procedure has no relation to democracy as known in ancient Greece.

Democracy in modern times has two basic defects: representatives do not require any qualifications to stand for election, neither intellectual nor ethical.

This is a very serious flaw as they are elected on the basis of a policy to be pursued, a policy that representatives are not compelled to uphold. Once they are elected the public has no longer authority over them as power has been transferred. This is amply displayed when democracies go to war without consulting the electorate, or seek imperialistic control of the territories of other nations. There is no reference to the general populace for authority to exploit colonial labour and resources.

Democracy today, with its entrenched party system of administration, is totally at variance with the original Greek model. Under this system loyalty to the party takes precedence over rationality and individual thought. The party hierarchy will not permit a member to stray from its committed policy. This is most apparent when the administration faces crisis periods: popular discontent, economic disaster, revolts and war. The ruling party then becomes despotic. The symptoms of a totalitarian state are then exhibited. The party is identified with the state and attacks are directed at the press, journalists, writers, academics and the Opposition in Parliament or Congress.

Criticism is regarded as treason. Extreme measures are taken in the name of democracy and the people. Newspapers and books are banned, television and radio stations controlled and information harmful to the party suppressed.

The first sign of a decay in administration evident in Parliament or Congress is when Opposition party members are vilified, traduced, defamed as unpatriotic and condemned for not working for the upliftment of the country. The rigidity of the party system does not tolerate criticism from within or without. From the chamber of parliament or Congress totalitarian intolerance spreads to embrace the entire state.

In the modern democratic party system of governance there are structures that appear to be independent: the Presidency, the Cabinet, the Legislature, the Judiciary. This is a delusion as the structures are under the control of the ruling party. The judiciary, consisting of magistrates and judges, are not only appointed and paid by the administration, but have no say in the declaration of war, corruption and unfulfilled general election promises. The ruling party's power is absolute in its control of finance. In order to maintain its power it will create a large army on the basis of unfounded threats to the sovereignty of the state. It will also seek the support of 'intellectuals' to buttress its hegemony by rationalisations and sophistry.

The party system of governance operates in all states, whether capitalist or communist. Slogans during elections such as 'The People Shall Govern' or 'The People Are Supreme' remain slogans without substance. To power-hungry politicians, whether individuals or collectives, constitutions mean little. They are often flouted by appeals to 'national emergencies' 'third forces' or 'foreign dangers'.

The UNO, since its formation after the Second World War, has flagrantly disregarded its Human Rights Charter. This is evident in the wars that member states, especially states that comprise the Security Council, have unleashed against weaker states. The Security Council, with its five permanent members, former imperialists, may be seen as an enlargement of the party system of administration, to control the world.

The ongoing crisis in the Middle East demonstrates this. America exercised its veto to prevent the UN peace-keeping forces from going to Palestine to stop the carnage. The other recent example is the Russian destruction of the city of Grozny in Chechnia and the vendetta against the population.

Modern democracy, that is, a representative system of government, can only work when it is upheld by rationality and ethical principles, and where the electorate has achieved a high level of discernment and judgement and will not accept deception.

As long as democracies function on the basis of partisan politics, we cannot hope to see a world free of strife, cruelty and agony.

Shareef Suhail received the following response:

'I read your interesting essay. I once stated at forums in Persepolis, Athens, Rome, Timbuktu, Hollywood, that the democratic system is the only one that presents an open political door for every citizen to aspire to become the president of a state. Citizens freely elect their leaders and deserve what they get. If they elect a Solon they get a Solon, if they elect a Bokasa they get a boa, if they elect a Reagan they get a deacon, and if they elect Nixon they get nix.

'You tell me that the citadel has been deconstructed stone by stone. Sadness overcame me when I learnt that. But that is the way of politicians. They always want to destroy the past so that only they are remembered. But I should not be sad over a citadel. Have they not been responsible for the death of millions of civilians during wars – Dresden, Hiroshima, Nagasaki, Cairo, Leningrad, Sarajevo, Baghdad, Grozny?'

XVIII

AFTER VISITING SHAREEF SUHAIL, Salman felt that he should visit a friend of his university days, Kamar, a lawyer. They had both studied for a Bachelor of Arts degree. After they graduated, Kamar decided to study law, and he had left for England with his parents. He had heard of Kamar at various functions and meetings of exiles in London when visitors from South Africa were also present. Kamar had acquired a reputation for defending those arrested for opposing repressive legislation such as the Group Areas (Ghetto) Act, and teachers who had been dismissed or subjected to punitive transfers by the education authorities. He was said to be the only advocate who undertook work without payment from those who could not afford legal fees. There was another reason why he wished to revive his acquaintance. He could be the man that destiny had selected to fulfill the third prophecy. If a man like Mr Khamsin whose education did not exceed high school level could be in parliament, what was there to exclude Kamar? In any case no qualifications were needed in democracies for anyone to be elected to political power; it all depended on ambition, influence, manipulation, cunning, and wealth, a powerful factor in all states.

He found Kamar's telephone number in the directory; he lived in the suburb of Lenasia. He telephoned Kamar and was pleased to hear his voice. Kamar said that he would be delighted to see him.

He went in his Mercedes Benz to the suburb which was about thirty kilometres south of the city. During the time he had been the Minister of Education he had visited schools there and the Teachers' Administration Centre.

He stopped at the street address given to him. He was surprised. It was a modest house compared with others he had seen along Nirvana Drive when he entered the suburb. He opened the gate, entered a well-kept garden and when he knocked at the door Kamar appeared. He had been an extremely handsome youth at university and still looked handsome, with sleek long black hair, bright eyes and a sculpted face. His frame was still slender. Kamar shook his hand and said: 'You have changed much, Salman, since our university days.'

'You know what state responsibilities can do.'

They sat down in the lounge.

'Especially after you have been given two cabinet appointments.'

'As a lawyer you know what work is involved with prisoners.'

'I can imagine your load.'

'Times have not been easy. Are you a bachelor?'

'My wife will soon be here. She is visiting a friend a few houses away. We shall have tea when she comes.'

The door opened and Zenobia entered, an aura of delicate perfume enfolding her. Salman stood up and saw a lovely tall woman before him, dressed in a two-piece pink costume, a pearl neckband, and hair coiled above her head. Kamar introduced her. As he stood beside his wife Salman saw that he was in the presence of an extremely happy couple.

'I read much about you,' Zenobia said, sitting down on the settee next to her husband, 'when you were in control of education. Kamar told me that you were together at university.'

'Yes, those were happy times, despite Apartheid. Youth is always a happy period.'

'Though not for everyone. Doctor Khan, will you have tea or coffee?'

'Please call me Salman. During week-ends and recess I try to forget status and official duties. I will have tea.'

Zenobia rose and went to the kitchen.

Salman and Kamar talked for a while about their university days, their lecturers, the forums where political discussions took place, the various vocal adherents of liberation movements.

Zenobia came with a tray of tea and cake and handed cups to Salman and Kamar.

'There is always much to say when friends meet after a long absence,' she said.

'Our university days were very exciting.'

'Zenobia was a teacher of English literature before transition,' Kamar informed his visitor.

'I wish I had met her when I was the Minister of Education.'

'You did good work,' Zenobia commended. 'But you upset teachers and principals when you threatened them with dismissal if they did not perform well. You were not aware of the collapse in education during the 1976 pupil revolt. Their slogan was "Liberation before Education".'

'Unfortunately I was not here. I did my best, but that went unappreciated. I tried to impose discipline.'

'That was necessary after the disorder.'

'There seems to be a relapse now.'

'Kamar and I were surprised when you were removed from your position. Perhaps you offended the Teachers' Union by the strict measures you applied. Perhaps they pressured the President.'

He had not thought of that possibility.

'How are you coping with your new portfolio?'

'I prefer not to talk about it.'

After some further conversation Salman decided to leave. He regretted that he had not made their acquaintance soon after his arrival in the country for he could have benefited from their advice. He was grateful that Kamar had not referred to his negligence in not visiting earlier.

'You must bring your wife when you come again,' Zenobia said to him at the gate.

He shook hands with Kamar and departed.

'His removal from the Education portfolio seems to have given him much pain,' Kamar said to his wife as they re-entered the house.

When Salman reached home Elizabeth was not in. The maid said that she had gone to the Khamsin home and would not be back till the evening.

He went into the garden and walked along the pathways. He stopped beside a clump of blooming irises and thought of Kamar and Zenobia. Kamar had given no indication that he wished to enter the world of politics. He was happy in his vocation and content with his wife and home. He had no desire to live in a mansion and no desire to acquire wealth. The serenity he had felt in Shareef Suhail's apartment seemed to pervade his home as well. They were men not driven by desire for status and power. They were outside the third prophecy. As for Zenobia, a voice within him had said when she entered: 'What an elegant woman she is.' She surpassed Elizabeth not only in beauty, but in courtesy, perceptiveness, quality of voice, attractiveness of personality. If he had such a woman his life would have been different. Her stately presence set her apart from Elizabeth and Allison. She had reminded him of the beautifully groomed film actresses of his youth: Catherine Hepburn, Greer Garson, and Ava Gardner. No wonder Kamar looked so well.

Such a woman had an important bearing on a husband's physical and mental well-being.

The world of politics, Salman felt, was where everything was determined by ambition: first to gain a seat in parliament, then to be a minister, then to be the vice-president and finally president. These positions were accompanied by privileges, financial rewards and renown. If there had been no third prophecy with its tantalising promise that he could be the saviour of a state in decline, he would have resigned and devoted himself to intellectual pursuits.

XIX

Y USUF EBRAHIM MADE AN APPOINTMENT with the President of
UMAC. He went to his home in the suburb of Rondebosch.

'Shaykh Sayid,' he said, sitting down opposite him in the
lounge, 'I have come to speak to you about Dr Salman Khan,
the Minister of Prison Services. I have discovered that he is a
fraud.'

'Fraud?'

'He does not have the academic degree he claims to have. He
never attended university.'

'You don't need any qualifications to be in parliament or the
Cabinet.'

'That's true. But I know more than that. He pretends to be a
Muslim. He is a dangerous atheist.'

'Tell me, brother Ebrahim, why are you against him? Has he
done you harm?'

'Yes. I went to see him after I was no longer in parliament. He
said I should resign from my party and join the Front. Then he
would get me a diplomatic post in Cairo. I did that but he has
not kept his promise.'

'You should know that politics is not about morality.'

'He is an atheist and hates you.'

'I have seen him in the mosque.'

'That's for show. He hates Muslims. I have discovered that.'

'There is no compulsion in religion. The Qur'an states that
clearly.'

'Your organisation should expose him.'

'Why should we?'

'You are against the administration.'

'Brother Ebrahim, understand. Ours is a fight against
criminals and drug-dealers.'

'Dr Khan has cut short prison sentences of criminals and
allowed them to go home. I can eliminate him for you. I have a
gun.'

'I think you should be patient. You have been in parliament and may get there again. In a few years there will be another election.'

'Shaykh Sayid, I cannot wait. I am in limbo now, limbo. You understand? Politics is my life.'

'Do something else.'

'I attacked the administration and its policies when I was in parliament. I need your assistance now. I want you to eliminate the traitor.'

'Your proposal means murder.'

'Exactly. This man is ambitious I tell you. He told me that the day he is President he will crush your organisation like an ant.'

'You should know that politicians say one thing before they are elected and do another when they are in power.'

'I have been in the liberation struggle long enough to know what is right. Take me into your organisation and you will see me in the vanguard against this corrupt administration.'

'This requires consideration, as there are no politicians in the organisation. In the meantime I think you should study religion.'

'I am religious enough.'

'Listen, Dr Khan is not your enemy. Politics is your enemy. Come to mosque five times a day and you will see matters clearly.'

'So you will not eliminate Dr Khan for me?'

'How can I do that to a brother Muslim?'

'Shaykh Sayid, you disappoint me.'

'You should go home and spend time with your family.'

'I have no family.'

'Then with your brothers and sisters.'

'I have none.'

'Then read the Qur'an and seek guidance from Allah.'

'He has abandoned me.'

'He never abandons a sincere believer. I think he has taken you out of politics to show you another way, a way that will bring you peace and happiness.'

A young lady came into the room with a tray on which were two glasses of orange juice and a tray of glazed fruit. She placed the tray on a small glass table, turned to the visitor, salaamed and left.

'Is that your daughter?'

'Yes.'

'I would like to marry her.'

'That is a sudden decision.'

'I admire her.'

Shaykh Sayid went out of the room and returned with his daughter. She was slender, tall, wearing a floral kaftan and a scarf.

'Mr Ebrahim says he wants to marry you.'

'He has only seen me a moment ago. He doesn't know me.'

'What's wrong with that? Others see each other every day for a year and when they get married are divorced the next day.'

'And others don't see each other, they are in purdah, and are divorced the next day,' she responded.

'You are clever. I need a clever wife.'

'You are bold, I don't need a bold husband.'

'My daughter,' Shaykh Sayid said, 'is at the university, studying psychology.'

'I want to marry a psychologist. She will know my mind.'

'I know it already, you are a hysteric, or a schizophrenic, or a paranoiac schizophrenic or a hysteric paranoiac schizophrenic.'

'What is your name, clever lady?'

'Mehroon.'

'Mayroon, a lovely name.'

'Not Mayroon. Mehroon. I do not wish to marry a man who cannot pronounce my name correctly.'

She turned and left the room.

'You have your answer, Mr Ebrahim,' Shaykh Sayid smiled.

'I will come again to win her. In the meantime Dr Khan must be eliminated from society.'

'Listen to me. You have been in parliament for five years ... '

'I have enough money to have him sent to hell by your organisation.'

'We don't need your money. You know the Qur'an says we must seek knowledge, and the Prophet said we should even seek it in China. Why don't you travel until the next election. See the Forbidden City, the Great Wall, learn the language. Go to Siberia, Afghanistan, India. See the Taj Mahal. Or study the poetry of Omar Khayyam, Attar, Sadi, Hafiz. Or take up art, drama, music, pottery.'

Ebrahim stood up and looked as if he was being attacked by a bee-swarm. He quickly left the room, leaving the door open as he rushed to his car in the street.

XX

SALMAN RECEIVED AN UNSIGNED letter which read:

'You who played no part in the liberation struggle against the white racists, a coward who stayed out of the country and did not return to defy the Herrenvolk are now a Cabinet Minister. Daily I sing the praises of the President, who realised your true worth which is that of a microbe, for having ejected you from the portfolio of Education and locked you in a prison without a window or light bulb. You will remain there until you die.'

Salman, feeling very upset, wondered who could have written it. He showed the letter to Mr Khamsin.
'I suspect Mr Ebrahim. You remember him?'
'Yes.'
'Ignore the letter.'
'It could be someone else.'
'No. He must be very bitter still for having lost his seat and not received a post in the Foreign Service.'
'Should I hand the letter to the police?'
'No, not now. You will receive another.'
After three weeks another letter arrived. It read:

'You call yourself a doctor. Doctor of what? You are a fraud. I have traced your history. I wrote to the registrar of the university where you claim you graduated. The reply is that if ever you return you will be arrested. Yes, you will be jailed in Alcatraz.'

Mr Khamsin commented: 'He will write another letter. He will spin a web around himself.'
Salman felt threatened and regretted he had not approached the Foreign Ministry to give Ebrahim a post. A man in a disturbed frame of mind was capable of harming him. The

letters evoked the misery he felt when his portfolio was wrenched from him.

Mr Khamsin's prediction was soon realised when he received a third letter:

'I have spoken to the editor of a Sunday newspaper. You will soon be exposed as a fraud. I have all the evidence. You will find yourself outside the locked doors of parliament, begging to get in. You bought your degree from a bogus institution in America, you cunning rogue.'

When Mr Khamsin read the letter, he said: 'The time has now arrived to begin our attack. Fax the letters to the Editor of *The Cape Herald* and tell him to print a statement from you.'

'Will the publicity be good for me?'

'The scoundrel has exposed himself. He will write another. Then we shall take our final step.'

Salman reluctantly faxed the letters. The next day there was an article on the first page of the newspaper about the 'poison letters from an anonymous source' to the Minister and a statement by him:

'The letters are a slur on my integrity and dignity and imply a threat to my person.'

The next day, when Salman and Mr Khamsin returned to Hotel Diaz in the late afternoon, the porter handed Salman a letter.

'Who delivered this?'

'A small boy.'

The letter was opened in the lounge. It was written in mirror-script. After Mr Khamsin transcribed it, it read: 'You shall die, you traitor. I shall throw your heart to the gutter rats of Cape Town.'

'It is time now to nail him,' Mr Khamsin said. 'Take all the letters tomorrow to Colonel Van der Ray of Intelligence and tell him to hunt him down.'

'You sure it is Ebrahim?'

'Who else? The mirror writing says it all. He threatened you in your office, didn't he?'

The next day Salman made an appointment with the Colonel.

He handed him copies of the letters and said that he suspected Ebrahim. He related to him the incident in his office.

'Minister, don't worry,' Van der Ray assured him. 'Tomorrow we shall set our hounds on his trail. I shall have him chased here and placed on the gridiron.'

'He cannot accept that he is no longer in parliament.'

'We will make him accept what we have in store for him.'

'Should he not be confined in an asylum?'

'Asylum? Let me interrogate him. When I finish with him he will wish he was a gutter rat.'

Salman left, feeling uneasy. As he drove away he looked several times in the rear view mirror of the car to see if he was being followed by his tormentor.

Salman did not receive another letter. After a month the news was broadcast in the media that Yusuf Ebrahim had shot himself in his hotel room.

He said to Mr Khamsin, 'I wonder why I had to become involved with a lunatic.'

'You will have to keep your balance in politics. We have to deal with human beings, not robots. You know the saying, "It takes all sorts to make a world".'

Mr Khamsin's reference to the proverb did not quell the disturbance within Salman.

A man had come to him for help and he had failed. He was a factor in his death.

XXI

SALMAN AND MR KHAMSIN WERE in the lounge. Elizabeth came in and said:

'Today another farmer and his wife have been murdered. This brings the total since transition to five hundred and one. What have you politicians done to stop the killing?'

They did not answer.

'This cannot go on. Politicians here do not seem to realise the value of farmers. There is always food on their tables and do not give a thought to those who provide it.'

'You are perfectly right in your concern,' Mr Khamsin said. 'The state must protect them.'

'The state has not the resources to protect them,' Salman said. 'They have to see to themselves.'

'Look at it in this way. The metropolitan area of Johannesburg has four million inhabitants. When they wake up in the morning there is milk and bread. Other basic foods, such as maize meal which is the staple diet of the poor, is available. There are also vegetables and fruit. Will the administration only wake up when four million starve?'

'Most of the farmers are whites,' Salman commented. 'They are vulnerable.'

'Whether white or black they must be protected.'

Mr Khamsin agreed. 'Yes, they have the experience and knowledge to produce food on a very large scale for the urban population, and need security. Perhaps if the death sentence had been retained we would have had fewer murders.'

'I disagree,' Salman said. 'The state had to be brought into conformity with the civilised states of the world.'

'Yes, you were very vocal about this from the beginning and stood with the former President on the issue. Muslims were against your stand.'

'I have not changed my view.'

'If it had been retained you would have had fewer prisoners and less work.'

'There is no evidence that the death sentence is a deterrent. It is a primitive barbaric practice that has no place in the modern world.'

'Would you say that the murder of the providers of sustenance is not barbaric?"

'It is barbaric, but we cannot stop it with another barbaric practice.'

'Thousands of women have been raped, including little girls. Look at the statistics. They are frightening. In a recent case fourteen school girls were raped and murdered by an individual in a suburb in our city.'

'The man has been arrested.'

'Yes. He will receive the same sentence as a man who rapes one.'

'He must be deranged.'

'Leave that topic,' Elizabeth intervened. 'There is a crisis and something must be done.'

'Elizabeth,' Mr Khamsin addressed her, 'there is a party in parliament, fortunately small, that believes that all land must be restored to the indigenous inhabitants. The administration does not hold that view. Ancestral land is being returned to those who were dispossessed, and state land offered to those who wish to do farming.'

'Unfortunately,' Salman stated, 'university students do not wish to study agriculture. They are for the humanities and the sciences.'

Mr Khamsin supported him. 'An urban dweller does not wish to lift a spade. Even the children of white farmers do not wish to follow tradition. One day we will have to import food.'

'Can this matter not be raised in parliament?' Elizabeth asked.

'We are in a minority. Our voices carry little weight?' her husband replied.

'Are there no far-sighted politicians? Even the former President remains silent on the murders.'

'The problem,' Mr Khamsin explained, 'is essentially both historical and psychological. Let me draw a contrasting parallel. When Indians arrived in this province in the late nineteenth century they had little knowledge of the English language. The majority of them had been farmers in India, but that vocation was denied them by the white rulers. They could not acquire land, and were confined in reservations. They were faced with challenges. So they took to hawking goods, progressed to little shops, then to larger ones. But the community looked ahead. The youth had to be educated. So they built their own schools, both secular and religious. Salman and I are in parliament today because of the difficulties they had to overcome. Now when this country was transferred into the hands of the indigenous people, there were no challenges to face. They found themselves in possession of a country with the best infrastructure on the continent, possessing great wealth. In such a situation there is no appreciation, foresight declines and we have what we have today.'

'Then there is not much hope for this country.'

'There is,' Salman countered. 'I believe the new emerging middle class will save it from ruin.'

'In the meantime there is decay, banks are looted, hijackers thrive and bureaucrats empty the treasury. And amidst poverty, and lack of health and educational resources, a provincial administration spends millions changing the names of towns and cities.'

'The country is going through a dark phase,' Salman said, 'but will recover.'

'When?'

'When the Muslim saviour arrives.'

'Why not a Christian one?'

'That was Mr Roma's prophecy. Do you recall?'

'There is nothing certain about a prophecy. Many have proved to be false.'

'Not all,' Mr Khamsin said. 'It is the nature of a prophecy to be enigmatic.'

'Perhaps the saviour will come after we all perish of hunger.'

'Don't be pessimistic,' Mr Khamsin consoled, 'I will speak to Mr Delanie, the Vice-President, and ask him to take up the matter of the protection of farmers with the Minister of Safety and Security. I am pleased you have awakened us.'

'Why not the President?'

'I have known Mr Delanie for many years, before my appointment. I will go with him to the President.'

After Elizabeth left the room Mr Khamsin said to Salman:

'Do not say in public that you consider the death sentence barbaric. You will antagonise Shaykh Sayid. Besides, you have now attended mosque and he considers you to be a Muslim.'

'Thanks, Ismail. I will observe your advice.'

XXII

S ALMAN WAS NOT AWARE THAT whenever Mr Khamsin came to his office he would bring a present for his secretary: a box of Swiss chocolates, a broach, a bracelet. He would say a few words to her in adoration.

'You look lovely today Allison' or 'You are the most charming person I have ever met.'

'Thank you very much,' she would reply, standing up, displaying her ripe body in a tight skirt. She would enter Salman's office and return, and hold the door open for him to enter.

On other occasions he would say: 'You look like a garden in bloom' or 'You are the queen among secretaries' or 'You should be in parliament.'

On a Friday Salman was away inspecting prisons in North-West Province. Mr Khamsin, knowing that he would not return until Saturday evening, went to Allison and said to her after handing her a gold pendant: 'Would you like to have breakfast and lunch with me tomorrow?'

'Why not? I will be delighted.'

She told him where she lived.

The next morning they went to the Sea View Restaurant.

'I am surprised that Salman does not appreciate your beauty.'

'His work is very demanding.'

'And what is life without pleasure?'

'A washed out shell on the beach.'

'How true.'

After breakfast consisting of orange juice, salmon, eggs, rye bread toast, lime marmalade and coffee, Mr Khamsin inquired: 'Where shall we go now? To your apartment?'

'Before we go there let us go up Table Mountain. I want to see the proteas.'

They went to the cableway station.

On the Mountain Allison said again, with some variation, the words she had used to charm Salman.

At noon they descended and went to the restaurant for lunch.

In the late afternoon, while enjoying tea with Allison on the balcony of her apartment, Mr Khamsin said: 'When I am a Minister in the Cabinet you will be my secretary.'

'How will you arrange that?'

'I can arrange many things. If I could not I would not be in parliament today. I deposed Shareef Suhail. Do you remember him?'

'He resigned.'

'There are many ways of making a person resign.'

'Will you depose Salman?'

'I don't want the prison portfolio. That is not for me or you.'

'Then what will be good for us?'

'You will see when the time comes.'

'You are very sure of yourself.'

'If I wasn't I would not have three wives.'

'Three wives?'

'And thirteen children.'

'In this age? I don't believe you.'

'You will meet them some day. And you will be my fourth wife.'

'You will have to pay a very high dowry,' she laughed.

'A mansion perhaps.'

'Of my very own?'

'That's a promise.'

XXIII

THE TIME ARRIVED FOR Mr Khamsin's eldest daughter, Farial, to marry. She had recently graduated with a Bachelor of Arts degree at the university. She was a woman with an unblemished fair complexion, soft luxuriant black hair which she kept coiled with two long plaits falling over her shoulders and two curls cascading on either side of her face. Her eyes were dark blue with long lashes; her nose gracefully proportioned and her lips like camellia petals. Her waist was extremely slender and always ornamented with belts and girdles. When she wore a semi-transparent sari in the evening she appeared like a houri who had strayed from paradisal gardens into a suburban mansion. Her fiancé, Khayyam, had recently qualified as an attorney. He came from an extremely wealthy family of merchants from the suburb of Laudium near Pretoria.

Mr Khamsin was determined to make the occasion one that would reflect his own affluence and his parliamentary status. The wedding would extend over two days and would take place during a recess so that he would have sufficient time to make all the necessary arrangements.

Soon the entire Khamsin household was engaged in planning and preparation. Salman and Elizabeth also assisted. Many hours were spent in deciding how to entertain guests for two days. No expense would be spared. Lists of guests were compiled: the chief guest would be the former President, followed by President Zara and the Vice-President, Mr Delanie. The names of MPs and ambassadors to be invited were recorded as well as the editors of women's magazines. The invitation card would be specially designed by an artist so that many guests would retain it as a memento. The menu cards to be placed before each guest would also be very elaborate.

Salman requested Allison's presence at the wedding. His friend agreed and said that he should invite her a week earlier to help his family with arrangements. Salman felt happy as he would be close to her daily.

'I think,' Mr Khamsin suggested, 'she should stay at my home rather than yours. You cannot say how Elizabeth might view having your personal secretary sleeping in your home.'

Salman telephoned Allison and she came by airbus. The two men went to the airport to meet her. The Khamsin family were pleased to have her in their home.

Two days before the wedding – it was to take place on a Saturday – three pavilions were erected in the gardens of the mansion. The caterers brought in tables, chairs, crockery, cutlery and everything else required for banqueting.

Cooks had been contracted to supply all the food, and confectioners a large variety of cakes and delicacies, both Eastern and Western.

During the evening before the wedding day, a banquet was held. Many members of the extended Khamsin family were present as well as Farial's friends dressed in elaborate Eastern garments. The pavilions were festooned with ribbon and glowing varicoloured lamps. There was music, singing of gazals, women dancers, and in the mansion Farial's hands and feet were adorned by a professional henna decorator.

The next day the guests started arriving at ten o' clock. A telegram came from the former President in which he stated that he could not attend the wedding because of 'domestic circumstances'. He would explain in a letter later. He wished the bride and bridegroom happiness. Mr Khamsin felt disappointed. But soon President Zara arrived with his African-American wife, Venus, and the mayor and mayoress of the city in a black Rolls Royce. They were welcomed by Mr Khamsin, flanked by Ministers, members of parliament and their wives.

President Zara's wife was a tall, well-groomed woman with light-brown hair and blue eyes inherited from her Irish mother. In the porch of the mansion she was introduced to Mr Khamsin's three wives and his children. She embraced and kissed them.

Venus, since her arrival with her husband from America, had kept herself aloof from all the women in parliament. She had acquired a Master of Arts degree at Berkeley University, had been a songstress and had retained her spoken English with its American accent. She despised women in parliament who wore beads as she considered them naive not to perceive that beads were objects with which the African continent had been purchased by Europeans. 'These women will never emerge from their slave mentality,' she told her husband. She did not sit with them in the lounge, but went straight into the mansion interior, embraced Farial, kissed her, examined her wedding gown and laughingly sprayed perfume over her.

Farial's trousseau, her wedding dress as well as her rose pink dress for the second day, and the dresses of her bridesmaids, had been designed by a specialist couturier from the House of Valmont.

The President, the mayor, Mr Khamsin, Salman and the Ministers sat in the men's lounge for a while, and then went to the pavilion reserved for them. Waitresses in blue blouses and tight blue skirts offered them varieties of fruit drinks. There were delicacies of all kinds.

Many guests had now arrived. Their limousines were parked in the street and in the parking area on the mansion grounds. Security guards were employed to protect them. Smartly dressed men and bejewelled women walked along paths and on the shrub-fringed lawn while photographic and video cameras were focused on them.

Farial and her two bridesmaids left in a hired convertible Rolls Royce to visit a beauty salon where their hair was set, make-up applied and their dresses fitted by the couturier. When they returned the guests stood along the driveway from the entrance gate to see them. Farial's wedding gown was made of white lace and satin, with a fully beaded bolero and a trailing veil. Her maids of honour wore jade dresses with gold embroidery.

Soon a helicopter was heard whirring above the Khamsin mansion. As it landed on a stretch of lawn guests gathered. The bridegroom and his two best men emerged. They were dressed in dark grey suits, white shirts and black bow ties. They were welcomed by Mr Khamsin and Khayyam's father who had come earlier by car from Laudium. The bridegroom and his best men were escorted to the pavilion reserved for males where they were introduced to the President and dignitaries.

At midday Mufti Suleiman arrived to perform the wedding ceremony. First, prayers had to be performed on a stretch of lawn in the far corner of the garden. After prayers everyone returned to the pavilion where the ceremony was to take place. Khayyam sat near the representative of the bride and two witnesses at a table facing the Mufti. The bride's representative was asked if she consented to the marriage and he said yes. Khayyam was then asked if he was willing to marry Farial and he said he was. The Mufti recited a prayer blessing the couple and the ceremony ended with the signing of the marriage register. There were congratulations and embraces and then it was time for feasting.

The menu consisted of a wide selection, ranging from a variety of starters to mutton roast garnished with herb-laden piquant sauces, steak, chicken, salmon, lobsters, prawns (spiced and grilled), specially baked naan with fennel seed, salads, desserts and sweetmeats.

A small stage had been erected.

There was music and two Moroccan women danced.

In the pavilion reserved for women Farial sat on a stage with her bridesmaids.

The waitresses were dressed in pink blouses and skirts with frilled crescent-shaped magenta aprons. Gorgeous saris and a variety of imported designer garments from India were worn by the women. There was the flash of jewellery and the redolence of floral perfume. The guests were entertained by women singers and dancers from Durban.

In the children's pavilion the waitresses were dressed in white tunics and there were circus performers to provide entertainment – jugglers, acrobats and clowns.

Feasting, music and conversation went on till the late afternoon when the President decided that it was time to leave. He was asked to stay on for supper, but he declined saying that he had eaten enough for two days. The mayor first addressed the guests and wished the bridegroom and bride happiness in their married life. Then the President delivered the following speech:

'Gentlemen, I feel very honoured to attend the wedding of the daughter of one of the most respected members of parliament. I have not in many years attended such a lavish banquet. I wish the bride and bridegroom a happy long life in this beautiful country of ours. Before I leave I should like to see the bride and wish her happiness.' There was applause.

Mr Khamsin and the bridegroom's father accompanied President Zara and the mayor to the women's marquee. They entered and went to Farial on the stage. He shook her hand and said that she was the loveliest bride he had ever seen. Then he lifted his hand to all the women in farewell.

The mayoress was ready to leave, but Venus said that she would like to stay over at the Khamsin residence till the next day. The President agreed, to the delight of Dr Khamsin's wives. He departed to return to his official residence in Cape Town in his private jet.

Feasting and entertainment continued till the late evening.

Khayyam and Farial went to the Midas Hotel to spend their first night.

The next day was another occasion for banqueting. Other entertainers arrived.

The bride and all the women guests were now attired in new garments and walked on the garden lawns displaying their beauty. Venus was given an Oriental full-flowing turquoise skirt with an embroidered waistcoat that displayed her navel and a long tasselled silk scarf to grace her right shoulder. She sang in the ladies' pavilion, recalling the eras of Josephine Baker, Eartha Kitt and Ella Fitzgerald.

Late in the afternoon everyone said farewell to Khayyam and Farial before they departed for Laudium where there would be a lavish reception for them.

On the following day they would take the plane to the island of Mauritius for a two-week honeymoon.

XXIV

M R KHAMSIN RECEIVED THE following letter as promised from the former President:

'Thank you for the invitation to the wedding of your most charming daughter, Farial. As you know the State, after my resignation, gave me a mansion in Orange Grove Park in East London. Why did they? I have pondered over this for many days and nights and at last have arrived at the understanding that it was to imprison me so that I could not leave it to regain my position as President. This was the secret motive of those who proposed that a mansion should be donated to me for my contribution to the liberation struggle. You will therefore appreciate that I cannot leave my prison even if I want to. They have cunningly appointed certain domestic servants to ensure that I do not venture out. I would first have to obtain the permission of the doorman, who is a sullen taciturn man, who pretends to be hard of hearing. He is completely unlettered so that I cannot even inscribe a wish to leave the mansion. He lets visitors in, but will not let me out. He sits the whole day and night on a bench in the porch, and even has his meals there, so that exit is impossible. If I were to tell him that I wished to attend a wedding, he would look at me as if I had asked him to commit suicide. His fixed sullenness, I have been told, was caused by his fiancé running away with her lover and with the diamond engagement ring he had bought with his lifesavings. Such a man has been placed by the authorities as the doorkeeper. You are aware that officials in public service today are more cunning than in Apartheid times. The oppressors that I had to tourney against used brutal force and I overcame them. But how does one overcome a man who is a pessimist?

'Even if I succeeded in convincing the doorkeeper to let me pass, I would be stopped by the two sentries at the gate. These sentries were former judo instructors who had been trained by

Nakamura, the famous Tenth Dan from Japan. Could I ever pass them without being tilted over in a second and find myself sprawled on the ground with a broken arm and my head concussed. What Nakamura also accomplished was to teach them his language, so that they have not only forgotten their native tongue, which is Greek, but also the English language. How can I ever communicate with them and tell them that I wish to attend a wedding. Not satisfied with the lethal power of their hands, they also carry two Second World War bayonets that would be used to stab me after the bullets are spent.

'Then there is the chauffeur of my gold-painted Rolls Royce, given to me by Sir Roland du Bois of the Chamber of Commerce. Every morning he takes the limousine out of the garage, which is a Persian carpeted wall-tiled room with a crystal chandelier, and spends the entire day polishing it. For diversion he spends his time looking in the fenders, flanks, windows and gleaming wing mirrors at himself dressed in his uniform, with gleaming brass buttons and a belt with a burnished bronze clasp. He will not enter the car to clean it inside without changing his uniform, a needless activity as there is not a speck of dust within. Then he will sit inside for many hours admiring the interior. The car has become his private possession and obsession. He also spends many hours going under the chassis and cleaning it. He hates dust as you and I hate oppressors. Whenever I come near the car he will place himself in my way and say, 'Do not come any closer. This car belongs to Her Royal Highness, Queen Victoria. When she visits this country I will drive her to my home in Rhodesia. Your shadow will stain the chrome-work.' He has a polished club that he keeps close by. As I do not wish to endanger my cranium, I withdraw. Once I asked him to take me for a drive and the stare he gave me was that of a Bengal tiger and that has prevented me from repeating the request.

'Then there are the two cooks. They are identical twins who spend their days preparing different meals for me and for all those employed in the mansion, including the two sentries at the gate. They claim to be the descendants of Paul Kruger. As you know he was a man who could fell an ox with one hand and kill a lion with the other, like Samson. He was the President who defied the might of the British Empire – a man beside whom I am insignificant. Have you visited his home in Pretoria? I suggest you go there and you will still feel his formidable presence in the interior. In fact the two monumental lions at the entrance gate will fill you with awe. At the back of the house is his horse carriage and his beautiful wagon, which has a letter box. One of these days I am going to tell this to the chauffeur to dent his pride. Kruger's private train coach, with gleaming furniture, also stands at the back on rails. Do you know where the Kruger gold coins are? Hundreds of treasure hunters from all over the world have been searching for a century in mountain caves along the railway line to Lourenco Marques. What they don't know is that the trove lies under the floorboards of the train coach. When you retrieve the coins – which I know you will do at night – please send me one afterwards as a memento.

'To return to the two cooks. They will not permit me to eat elsewhere and have threatened that should I leave the mansion they would continue to pile all meals on my dining table so that on my return I would have to consume all the food at one sitting. They will tie me to my chair so that I cannot escape. You can imagine what the consequences would be to my frail constitution. Besides, there are thousands of starving children in this country and I would not like to see the food wasted. I can assure you that you would not want to encounter these women in a forest or a plain. They will stand on each side of you, grip your legs between their massive thighs, take your arms, place them behind your back, push them upwards and break them like twigs. Sometimes I have thought of proposing to them that they should come with me to Spain where I would get them engaged as matadors (is there a feminine form of the word?). In the bull ring they would fearlessly face the beast, wrench off its horns, go beneath its legs, and carry it around the arena to the applause of thousands of spectators. One day when you visit me I will ask you to speak to them about my proposal.

'As for the four maids who see to the maintenance of the household, they are always dressed like nurses and are as rotund as the nurses at our State hospitals who consume large quantities of food prepared for patients. They have threatened that should I leave the mansion even for an hour they would all get into my bed.

'I do not relish the prospect of four women in my bed, no, not a single one, as I have been a bachelor all my life.

'There is also my assistant gardener, a Roman, who is always dressed in the black cassock of an ecclesiastic. He carries an ancient Bible in red buckram as though to ward off evil spirits that he believes inhabit my garden. I can tell you he is no Vatican ecclesiastic, but a spy appointed by the state to watch over me as I prepare the soil, plant seeds and harvest vegetables. I learnt much about gardening in Russia, while other exiles spent their time revelling like Rasputin and pursuing street women. Now this spy never leaves me while I labour.

When I bend down he bends down; when I lift a spade to turn the soil over he does the same; if I scatter seeds he will imitate my action. When I tell him he should stop behaving like my shadow, he repeats my words, then opens the Bible and begins to read the Book of Job. I wish the State had appointed a real spy, the kind you see on television, with dark glasses, hiding behind tree trunks, crawling under hedgerows, or concealed in a ditch. That would be exciting. But the Roman has no sense of adventure. I have often thought of plunging a fork into his ribs, but have refrained as I am certain he has a suit of armour under his cassock and he will only laugh derisively at me when the fork breaks against tempered steel. On Sundays he preaches to the domestic staff under a chestnut tree, petrifying them, as he reads an encyclical that proclaims all human beings must experience hell fire for a thousand years after death before they can enter paradise and appreciate its supernal bliss. I stand at an upper storey window and see him point his right hand at me to show the congregation that there stands the rebel against God. I have told the staff many times that the ecclesiastic is a spy in disguise, but do you think they will listen to me? They look at me with dire disdain as though I had fathered Satan. I long for a knight of King Arthur, Sir Gawain himself, to come and rescue me from captivity.

'My dear Ismail, I am sure that you will now appreciate my position. I cannot come out. I would have loved to attend the wedding of your beautiful daughter whose name, Farial, I repeat over and over again because of its musical tone. How I regret that I could not enjoy the delicious food provided for the guests and not see the dancing girls with open midriffs. I plead to you to speak to the hundreds of officials that stand between me and freedom. If I am ever released – I am not hopeful as officials are noted for their intransigence, without which they would lose what is most precious to them, a sense of power – I shall come over and spend a few days with you. We shall visit Farial and her husband. Do give them my best wishes for a happy married life.'

When Mr Khamsin came to the end of the letter he believed he understood why the President had resigned without informing anyone of his intention. He felt that the letter would not only be of interest to historians, but to psychologists and psychiatrists, and locked it in his safe.

XXV

THE INQUEST COMMISSION, established after transition to democracy, continued its mandate to listen to the evidence of the myrmidons of the former regime – officials of administrative bureaus, police officers, secret intelligence agents, undercover 'hit men', informers and others employed to annihilate the leading figures of liberation movements – in order to grant amnesty to the deserving. Many volunteered to give evidence as those who refused, in terms of the mandate, would be arrested and arraigned.

When the murder of Rosalind Sands was placed on the agenda of the Commission at its hearing in Johannesburg, Salman and Elizabeth decided to give evidence against the man who had sent her a letter-bomb while she had been engaged as a lecturer at the University of Dar-es-Salaam. Salman knew her during his school days in the city, and he and Elizabeth had worked closely with her in the Socialist Party as well as in other organisations that wished to end white racist tyranny. They informed the Commission of their intention and were called to a hearing under the chairmanship of Justice Bloom in the Supreme Court.

Justice Bloom was assisted by four assessors. The man who had applied for amnesty sat at a table on the right of the court room. His hair was grey, his facial features that of a mild, good-natured man. Salman and Elizabeth saw for the first time the man who had killed Rosalind. Justice Bloom asked Mr Corlet to present argument for seeking amnesty. He read the following from a sheet of paper before him:

'Your worship, I was engaged by the Central Bureau of State Security and assigned to the 'White Knights' section. Our task was to eliminate enemies of the state, men and women who were involved in conspiracies to overthrow the state by violence or propagation of violence. I was sent to England on

113

1970 to spy on the activities of South Africans who belonged to subversive organisations in the country, and had fled. I together with three others kept a careful watch on their movements and the meetings they attended. I examined the newspapers and kept a record of the articles they wrote. We considered Rosalind Sands a dangerous communist and we singled her out as a target. She spoke at various meetings, in Hyde Park and elsewhere. She was a member of the Socialist Party. Her view was that a violent revolution was necessary to destroy white power. My two partners, now deceased, assisted me. We sent regular reports to the Central Bureau of State Security and they ordered us to take action against Rosalind Sands. We decided to place an explosive device outside her home, but she soon left England for Dar-es- Salaam. We discovered that she had taken a post at the university. My colleagues and I then decided to send a letter bomb to her.'

He was then cross-examined by Mr Dupont, a lawyer that Rosalind's husband had engaged.

'When did you join the Central Bureau of State Security?'
'In 1963.'
'Why did you decide to join the Bureau?'
'I was out of work.'
'What work did you do?'
'I was a clerk in a business firm.'
'You had no other reason to join?'
'No.'
'What were your political views at that time?'
'I had none.'
'You did not hate non-Europeans, people not white?'
'No.'
'When you joined and learnt what your mission was, you did not think it was immoral?'
'They paid me and I felt satisfied.'

'When you were sent to England and you listened to Rosalind's speeches and read the articles she wrote, did she propagate violence against the South African government?'

'Yes.'

'Have you any articles by her to prove that?'

'No. This happened a long time ago.'

'Did you not think that to substantiate your request for amnesty you should go to England and obtain the articles from newspapers?'

'No.'

'If Rosalind had not left England would you have placed a bomb near her home?'

'Yes.'

'She and her husband could have been killed?'

'Yes … possibly.'

'You did not feel that that would be wrong as her husband was not a South African citizen?'

'My colleagues did not think so and I did not.'

'Who sent the instructions from the CBSS that you should kill Rosalind?'

'I think it was Colonel Calvin who has been granted amnesty.'

'Did you regret what you did?'

'Yes.'

'In what way did you show your regret after you learnt she had died?'

'I don't understand the question.'

'What did you do to show regret? Did you write a letter to her husband?'

'No.'

'Did you write a letter to him after transition?'

'No.'

'Can you recognise him in the audience?'

'Yes,' he said, after looking.

'You did not show any regret, yet you are applying for amnesty?'

'It was a political action on my part. I carried out orders as a White Knight.'

Salman was questioned next.

'Dr Khan, did you know Rosalind Sands?'

'Yes.'

'Please inform the Commission.'

'I met her for the first time when I was attending school in Fordsburg, a suburb in this city. In 1950, when I was in my final year, she lectured to a group of pupils on socialism. I attended her lectures. She elevated my social awareness of conditions in this country.'

'What was your impression of her?'

'She was a very intelligent woman, deeply concerned about the repression of the dispossessed proletariat.'

'What did she tell you about socialism?'

'She said that it was a political ideology that preached equality of opportunity without race or class prejudice and that a socialist state would eradicate poverty. She also enlightened us on the political ideas of Karl Marx and Lenin.'

'What else can you tell the Commission?'

'I met Rosalind Sands again when I was in England at Cambridge University. She came there to speak to students about conditions here. After I had completed my studies I joined the Socialist Party of South Africa, of which she was the founder. I later became the president.'

'Did you listen to her speeches at public meetings?'

'Yes, I did.'

'Did she propagate violence as a means of overthrowing the South African state?'

'She never did.'

'Did you read the articles she wrote in newspapers?'

'Yes. In fact she disagreed with those exiles who advocated violence. She felt that such acts could lead to the death of innocent people who disapproved of the Apartheid regime. She contended that it was a mistake to believe that all whites were racists.'

116

'Thank you, professor Khan.'

Elizabeth was questioned next. She said that she had been a member of the Socialist Party with her husband and she too had not heard Rosalind Sands propagate violence as a means of dislodging the Apartheid administration. Counsel then questioned Mr Corlet again.

'You have heard the evidence of Dr. Khan and Mrs Khan. They have both stated that they neither heard about nor read articles by Rosalind Sands advocating violence. In your written statement you have stated that she did.'

He did not answer.

'Your Worship,' advocate Dupont addressed Justice Bloom, 'I wish to submit articles written by Rosalind Sands that appeared in newspapers in England for examination by the Commission.'

He went over to the judge and handed him a file. He then resumed cross-examination.

'What standard did you complete at school, Mr Corlet?'

'Standard eight.'

'Now should the Commission believe your evidence or that of Dr Khan and his wife?'

He did not answer.

'You sent the letter bomb with your colleagues, knowing that the lady advocated peaceful change in this country. I put it to you that you are not telling the truth.'

'I had to carry out orders.'

'If you did not?'

'I would have been dismissed.'

'You should have resigned instead of carrying out an evil act. You were in no way politically compelled to commit a crime.'

Mr Dupont then addressed the Commission and said that Mr Corlet should not be granted amnesty. There had been no political constraint for his act. The only loss he would have sustained was dismissal.

Justice Bloom adjourned the hearing till the next day. He would evaluate evidence with the assessors before delivering judgement.

Salman and Elizabeth were pleased to meet Rosalind's husband, who had arrived from London the previous day.

They took him home and spoke about earlier times.

The next day Justice Bloom delivered judgement:

'Mr Corlet, your application for amnesty has been rejected by the Commission. Your evidence that Rosalind Sands advocated violence to overthrow the former Apartheid state is a fabrication. At no stage in the proceedings did you show any sign of remorse nor did you make a plea to that effect in your written submission. A record of the evidence presented will be sent to the Minister of Justice, who will institute further proceedings against you.'

At home Salman said to Elizabeth:

'The Commission, when other judges have presided, have granted amnesty to officials of the previous regime. Those who issued orders are also accomplices. They have escaped punishment.'

'I hope Mr Corlet is imprisoned for life.'

Salman was filled with profound sadness. He went into the garden and pondered why evil so often triumphed over good. Was the clemency offered to the previous principals of the regime and the assassins they hired, was it good or was it a compromise with evil? He could find no answer.

XXVI

THE TEN MUSLIM MEMBERS OF parliament received a similar letter from Saleem Anwar Sayid which read:

'You are aware of the crisis in Bosnia where Muslims are being attacked by infidel Serbs, supported militarily by the state of Yugoslavia. They have embarked on a campaign of 'ethnic cleansing', committing heinous atrocities against men, women and children. Many homes and mosques have been set on fire and the Holy Qur'an desecrated. The Security Council of the UNO have consented to the annihilation of Muslims by imposing arms sanctions on Bosnia. This criminal act by former imperialists reneges on the Charter of the UNO and the Universal Declaration of Human Rights. We intend to march to the consulates of America, Britain and France to demonstrate our condemnation of the world Organisation's failure to protect the Muslims of Bosnia. We request your presence on 20 September.'

'Salman,' Mr Khamsin reflected vocally, 'Shaykh Sayid's letter places us in a dilemma.'

'Yes, it does.'

'If we do not attend, we will be branded as being indifferent to the fate of Muslims in Bosnia. If we attend the administration will accuse us of supporting "fundamentalists" and "terrorists".'

'Do you know who will attend and who not?'

'I will speak to each one tomorrow.'

The next day Mr Khamsin informed Salman that only Mr Bengali had said that he would take part in the demonstration.

'The viper. If only he attends we shall be hated. The imams at the mosques will eject us. The viper will gloat.'

'If we all stay away we could offer an explanation.'

'Ismail, you will have to find a way to redeem us.'

'I will convene a meeting in the hotel lounge tomorrow night. We must arrive at unanimity.'

Mr Khamsin spoke to the other eight members of parliament and they agreed to meet in the hotel. When they arrived he addressed them:

'Gentlemen, we are in a predicament. We all feel the anguish of the Muslims in Bosnia and we would all like to march in solidarity to demonstrate our condemnation of the Security Council resolution. I do not have to tell you of the view our administration holds of UMAC. We either all join the march to the consulates or we all stay away. What is your opinion?'

Mr Bengali said:

'If I do not join them how shall I face the congregation in the mosque? I do not go to mosque on Fridays only, but every day.'

Mr Mohamed, a former lawyer, incensed by the implied slur on them by the latter statement, countered:

If your loyalty is to UMAC then you should resign.'

'My loyalty is to God.'

'Then what are you doing in parliament? It is not a mosque.'

'Gentlemen.' Mr Khamsin intervened. 'Let us not get bogged down in recrimination. We have a dilemma to solve.'

No one spoke for a while. Salman looked at Mr Bengali, who stared fiercely at Mr Mohamed.

'Gentlemen, I have a proposal,' Mr Khamsin said. 'I will approach the President and ask him to publicly express regret at the situation in Bosnia and state that at the request of the Muslim members of parliament he will permit humanitarian aid to be sent.'

'Would that be sufficient to absolve us from joining the demonstration?' Mr Mohamed inquired.

'I think so. We must all stay away. Will that satisfy you, Mr Bengali?'

He did not answer, still smarting at Mr Mohamed's verbal thrust.

Several others pressed him to agree as the proposal was reasonable. He remained silent.

'We could also,' Mr Khamsin said, 'make a financial contribution to a fund that has been established by Muslims in Durban to aid the victims in Bosnia.'

Mr Khamsin appealed to Mr Bengali to reconsider and he agreed.

The next day Mr Khamsin went to speak to Mr Delanie, the Vice-President, and explained to him the dilemma they faced. Thereafter the two men went to the President's office. The President obliged by accepting the proposal. In the evening Salman commented: 'Ismail, only you could have saved us and you have. Where did you acquire your astuteness?'

'Many people have a simple view of the world of commerce. They think it is only about making money. It is more than that. You gain an insight into human behaviour, the motive springs of statements and actions. Sometimes it is necessary to compromise, sometimes to bend people to your own advantage. It is a world where the astute survive. What I have learnt in commerce I apply to politics.'

'I wish I had learnt that in the lecture halls of Cambridge.'

On the day before the UMAC demonstration, the President duly made his statement expressing the administration's concern about the situation in Bosnia and that 'peaceful protest demonstrations were permissible in terms of democratic practice' and further that 'at the request of the Muslim members of parliament', humanitarian aid could be sent.

'I am going to attend the demonstration,' Mr Khamsin surprised Salman.

'What?'

'I want to see what happens at the American consulate. You must come with me. We shall go as observers.'

The next day Mr Khamsin and Salman went by car towards the American embassy and parked a short distance away. Soon the demonstrators arrived from the opposite direction, carrying placards which read: 'The Security Council Supports Genocide', 'The UNO is ruled by Imperialists', 'Bosnia Will Overcome'.

The demonstrators stood before the gate of the consulate and chanted: 'America supports Serb murderers.' Then an American flag was set on fire and a loud shout in unison erupted: 'Stop the war in Bosnia.'

Five trucks arrived carrying policemen with shields, guns and batons. The demonstrators found themselves surrounded and attacked as tear gas canisters exploded.

Mr Khamsin quickly started the car, reversed, and drove away as the demonstrators scattered in all directions.

'This is terrible,' Salman disapproved. 'Why have the police attacked them?'

'The state has no love for UMAC.'

The next day the police action was criticised by journalists who had accompanied the demonstrators. Several journalists had their television cameras smashed. The journalists stated that the attack was unprovoked and that apart from the burning of the American flag no damage had been done. The Police Commissioner stated that he had received information that the demonstrators were going to storm the consulate and set it on fire. The police action had prevented damage and the possible murder of the American consul and his staff.

Saleem Sayid strongly condemned the attack and said that the demonstrators had not damaged the consulates of Britain and France and had no intention of damaging the American one. He also said that he saw no difference between the old regime and the new one.

Mr Khamsin told Salman: 'Now whether the Muslim members of parliament were present or not will not be an issue.'

He did not tell Salman that he had informed the Commissioner a day before that he had received secret information that the demonstrators planned to storm the American consulate premises and set it on fire.

A week later Salman received the following letter from Saleem Sayid:

'Please meet me tomorrow on Table Mountain at 10 o'clock. I shall be waiting for you on the right of the cableway terminal, about five hundred metres away.'

He felt vulnerable. The mosque in Chapel Street had been a sanctuary. On the mountain he would be alone with a man who was prepared to challenge the state.

'What does the letter say?' Mr Khamsin inquired, seeing Salman looking crestfallen.

Salman handed him the letter.

'You will have to meet him.'

'Why does he want to see me again?'

'You will know when you meet him.'

'Perhaps because of the police attack?'

'Possibly.'

Salman noted that Mr Khamsin looked a little troubled. He poured tea and said:

'Let us not speculate what Saleem Sayid will say to you. If he has a request we will consider it when you return.'

The next day Salman kept the assignation.

Saleem Sayid extended his hand to him when he reached him and salaamed.

In the bright sunlight he looked even more impressive than when he had met him in the mosque. He was dressed in a long robe with a peacock-blue sheen and a white satin turban. Behind him lay the Atlantic Ocean.

'Brother Salman, can you tell me who informed the Police Commissioner that we intended to attack the American consulate?'

'I don't know, Shaykh Saleem,' he answered timidly.

'We know. He is a member of parliament.'

Salman remained silent.

'Where were you when the attack occurred?''

He felt petrified.

'We know that too, brother Salman. But we will not go into that. What I want you and your friend Mr Khamsin to do is to

123

speak to Mr Reed of Victory Prison and tell him to allow our four Muslim brothers to be released from every Friday evening until Sunday night so that they can be with their families.'

Saleem Sayid's mention of Mr Khamsin was an intimation that his knowledge of the attack on the demonstrators at the American consulate was all-embracing.

'I will see what I can do.'

'The Merciful and the Compassionate will assist you. Go now with my salaams.'

Salman hurried away. When he reached the hotel he told Mr Khamsin:

'He knows everything. On the day of the demonstration we were seen.'

'Did he mention my name?'

'Yes. I think he suspects us for having informed the Commissioner.'

'We were foolish. We should not have held that meeting here. His postman and informer is here.'

Salman then told him of the request.

'That is not a request. It is a command we will have to carry out.'

'Will Mr Reed agree?'

'You must tell him that releasing them during week-ends is part of the administration's scheme of alleviating overcrowding in prisons and has been endorsed by the President.'

'That will be unprecedented. They have been sentenced.'

'You are the Minister. Changing conditions require different strategies. They are being released for good behaviour and such concessions can apply to others as well. Salman you are in authority and nobody can question you.'

'I will do as you say.'

'Shaykh Saleem is a man of God. We must in future be very careful of our relationship with him.'

XXVII

SALMAN EXTENDED AN INVITATION FOR lunch at his home to Shareef Suhail and Kamar and Zenobia. After his visit he wished to deepen his relationship with them.

In times of difficulty or when he needed advice on crucial state matters he could resort to them. Kamar had been his friend at university and there was much pleasure to be derived in the company of one who had been a contemporary during youth.

They arrived on Sunday at the gate of his mansion soon after noon. The sentry announced their arrival over the inter-communication system and Salman went out to meet his guests in the driveway. Shareef Suhail and Kamar were dressed in open-necked shirts and pants and Zenobia in a floral kaftan. Her hair was gathered and ornamented with a pearl-encrusted clasp. Her earrings glittered with amber gems and her perfume smelt delightful. The presence of friends filled Salman with delight, delight that he had not experienced often since his demotion.

The visitors were not surprised at their host's large mansion. Since transition many politicians had acquired wall-enclosed large properties in former white suburbs, and these were guarded by sentries at gates, elaborate electronic security systems, and motorised patrols that could be summoned by the press of a button.

Salman introduced Shareef to Kamar and Zenobia. 'We are old friends,' Kamar said.

'Friends?'

'Yes. I defended Shareef in court during the Apartheid days. Unfortunately I failed.'

They walked towards the open doorway of the mansion and entered the lounge. Elizabeth came in and she was introduced to the guests. She had heard of Shareef as his resignation from parliament had been broadcast on television and radio, and reported in newspapers. Her husband had also told her of his visit to him and to Kamar and Zenobia in Lenasia. She did not stay long with the guests as she had to supervise the maids preparing lunch.

'Tell me more about your defence of Shareef,' Salman asked Kamar.

'Shareef wrote an article for a paper called *Eastern Times* in which he stated that a revolt became necessary when a state became oppressive, especially when oppression was racial.'

'Yes,' Shareef agreed, 'but I also wrote, perhaps unwisely, that taking up arms was a civic duty and that everyone who was conscious of injustice should support those involved in active resistance and provide them with material aid.'

'Shareef,' Kamar continued, 'was charged with incitement to promote a violent revolution and found himself imprisoned on Dragon Island.'

'I am sorry to have spoilt your record of successes.'

'Don't write anything on politics in the future,' Kamar advised. 'I don't want to fail a second time.'

'Good came from your failure. I spent five years reading and writing.'

'Stay with history and philosophy,' Zenobia advised, 'and you will be safe. Even democrats can become autocrats.'

'Not in our state now,' Salman observed. 'It is non-racist now and everyone has the constitutional right to freedom of speech.'

'Zenobia distrusts all politicians,' Kamar said.

'I hope she trusts me?' Salman said, smiling at her.

'If I did not I would not have accepted your invitation.'

'Well said,' Salman commented laughingly.

'Why did you,' Zenobia inquired, 'when you were the Minister of Education remove Art and Music from the school curriculum?'

'You know that this is the age of technology and the idea was to concentrate on subjects that would provide pupils with knowledge to pursue lucrative careers later.'

'That deprived pupils of aesthetic appreciation and pleasure.'

Elizabeth came in and announced that lunch was served. They went to the dining room. Elizabeth had the cook prepare an array of dishes – she had learnt much from Mr Khamsin's wives – and everyone enjoyed the meal.

After lunch Salman said that they should all go to the gazebo in the garden where they would have tea.

After tea Zenobia said to Elizabeth: 'You have a lovely garden. Do you attend to it yourself?'

'No. The Landscape Gardening Contractors send their work-men every month and I supervise.'

'Can we take a walk?'

'Come.'

They went along a brick-paved path that skirted the swimming pool and then went towards parterres of flowers and shrubs.

While the ladies were away, conversation in the gazebo continued. Salman succumbed to the temptation to ask his guests about their opinions on the future of the country. In what direction did they see it going?

'That is an extremely difficult question to answer,' Shareef said. 'Who could prophesy, say in the eighties, that the previous regime that was in total control of the country, with a military force unmatched on the continent, would decide to cede power.'

'Yes,' Kamar supported. 'That surprised us.'

'The exiles did much to make Western countries exert pressure. There was disinvestment.'

'The old regime,' Kamar said, 'could have gone on for a long time. Neither the UNO nor European countries contemplated sanctions.'

'We are talking of the past,' Salman said. 'A prophet before the second election predicted that we would go through a dark phase. Do you remember, Shareef?'

'I remember. Mr Roma said that during the television panel discussion.'

'I remember too,' Kamar said. 'He also predicted that a Muslim would one day be the president. Rather a strange prediction from an African traditionalist.'

'I have not given much thought to that,' Shareef responded.

'And I have been puzzled since then,' Salman confessed. Can such a prophecy be fulfilled?'

'Not likely,' Kamar said. 'There are not many followers of Islam among blacks.'

Salman, throughout his mental tussle with the prophecy had never thought that Mr Roma's prophecy could apply to a convert. There was no convert in the political arena that had yet appeared as a distinct personality.

'Events in the political world are not predictable,' Shareef said. 'The forces that control politics are ambition, power and finance, often working in collusion. Religion is an outsider.'

'I agree with you,' Kamar said. 'And that is where I come in. I would soon be out of work if politicians and financiers acted in ways that are morally consistent at all times.' There was amusement.

'Shareef,' Salman inquired,' what is your opinion of Shaykh Sayid? Does he want a fundamentalist state based on Islamic law?'

'His organisation has emerged because of the lack of disciplinary power by the state to control criminal gangs. I don't think he wants to subvert the administration.'

'He is admired by many for his courage. Could he be president some day?'

'Not likely. If opposition continues by his organisation and by others in the future, such as the trade unions, the administration will become increasingly authoritarian and perhaps despotic.'

'I read,' Kamar told Salman, 'the evidence you and your wife presented against Mr Corlet to the Inquest Commission.'

'I hope he will be jailed. Many have been granted amnesty who do not deserve it."

128

'Yes,' Kamar agreed, 'a precedent has been set that political crimes are different in nature from civil crimes.'

'That is a violation of equity and justice,' Shareef remarked.

The ladies returned. The group then discoursed on various other topics until the late afternoon, when they parted.

XXVIII

SALMAN DECIDED TO VISIT the former President. He had forgiven him for not having taken him into his confidence before his resignation and for not having ensured that his successor would retain him in his portfolio. He felt that, while conversing during the visit, he would be able to discover the reason for his resignation. Perhaps he had been impelled by a metaphysical force. He would also like to recall the time they had worked together during the negotiation with the white aristocracy to establish the new era in the country's history and question him about how he viewed the present and the future of the republic. He must have thought much during the past two years and would be able to offer him some beneficial advice.

Allison made an appointment for him and one morning he took the airbus to East London.

At the airport he hired a taxi and was soon at the gate in Orange Grove Park. The sentry at the gate was expecting him. When he reached the entrance the doorman allowed him in and he entered a spacious lounge. The former President, who was slightly below his visitor in height, came in saying, 'Salman, Salman, how often have I thought of you.'

They shook hands and sat down.

His hair had been dyed black and made sleek by the hair-dresser. His Egyptian-contoured lean face was clean-shaven, his deep-set eyes were bright. He was wearing brown pants, a short-sleeved cream shirt and a pale yellow cravat with a leaf pattern that gave him a sprightly appearance.

'You are looking very well,' Salman complimented.

'Exile in Russia did me good. I walked in the fields, snow, woods.'

'And from there you controlled the liberation struggle.'

'Those were wonderful days. The past. How can I forget. I was treated like a hero. Many comrades came to the land of Lenin, Tolstoy, Marx.'

Was his memory failing? Salman thought.

'You know, the past is always better than the present. I worked in a gold mine. Drilling. Lifting gold-bearing rocks. Filling railway wagons. I was strong. Salman, you should have seen me.'

He laughed.

'Yes, the old days. They were good. The day I was elected President of the Front in Gandhi Hall in Fox Street, Johannesburg, was the greatest day of my life. In the early years the police did not trouble us. Meetings were held, strategies planned. There was friendship, the joy of companions in the struggle.'

'That must have been an exciting period.'

'Yes, man, there is nothing like planning to overthrow a powerful state. You are a few. You are weak. No money. No guns. Only pens, and how we made the government shake!'

He laughed.

'I wish I could return to the old days. I lived in Sophiatown, Newclare, Alexandra. There was excitement. Doors were open, everyone friendly. There were Indian shops at every corner. They gave credit and we paid. Do you remember the cafes? The drinks, orange, lime, raspberry, in water fridges? And there were the bioscopes. Reno, Odin, Plaza, Rio. I saw *Zorro* there. Tyrone Power, Errol Flynn, Judy Garland. The actors and actresses were our friends. We spoke about them. My favourite, John Wayne. He taught me to wear a cravat. Did you see *Stage Coach*? Hey, man, that was a great movie.'

'You are famous today.'

'Today, yes, tomorrow, no. I will be remembered on a piece of paper. A name. Not John Wayne. Get his video today and you will see him. Alive. Handsome. Talking to his woman. Gail Russell. Using his six-shooters. Riding like a king on his horse.'

'Yes.'

131

'You should have seen me. I had a Buick. Shining, chrome all round. Gangsters in Sophiatown and Alexandra gave way when I drove in. I wish I had that car today. Did you know Gool?'

'Yes. He lived in Fordsburg where I lived.'

'Handsome, I tell you. Film star. Chicago man. Sharp brain. Club in High Road. We went there. What food came from his kitchen! Do you know that he took part in a passive resistance campaign. Went to jail. His car, a Farina Spider. In the street people would stand around. There was joy, Salman, I tell you there was joy.'

'Yes.'

'Do you remember the Lyric in Loverswalk? Saw *Bad Day at Black Rock* there. Spencer Tracy. He was a man.'

'And did you see *Samson and Delilah* at the Majestic? Victor Mature, handsomest of men, and Hedy Lamarr, beauty of beauties. And George Sanders, king of the Philistines, master of spoken English.'

'Yes.'

'Do you know liquor was prohibited to us? The whites, that was the best thing they did. If they had abstained and given us all the liquor they would have been in power today.'

He laughed.

'Those days are gone, Salman, gone for ever. Don't talk to me about today. Here am I. Alone. When I am invited overseas I go. I stay in five-star hotels. I make speeches. There are banquets. Honours. Am I happy? Forget it. I long for the days when life was worth living.'

'Unfortunately I was away in Cambridge.'

'You missed everything. Meeting, conspiring, keeping away from the police. Printing a newspaper. When they banned it, another. When they banned that, another and when they banned that still another. And the leaflets: "Rise Up!", "Throw off your Chains!", "Be Free!" Can you appreciate the joy of that? We worked with Indians. Real politicians in Adam's Arcade, between Market and Commissioner Streets. There was a restaurant there. O what food! When I returned I went to look. Broken down. A ten storey building had taken over. That building was history. You know some people have no sense of history. Lenin, Stalin, Marx. Their statues smashed. I will never go back to Russia.'

'You may be invited to visit.'

'Let me tell you, Salman, when you get what you want joy vanishes.'

'What about the future?'

'I don't want to talk about It. The past was real. I am going to write a book about those days. Write about today and no one will read it. The days of the struggle were the best days of my life.'

'Will you write about your youth?'

'My father died when I passed standard eight. I went down the mine to support my mother. After three years I returned to school and went on to become a teacher. After ten years I entered the political ring. The struggle gave strength, moral strength. Today? Everything is easy. Hard work? No, not for us. We are free. There was no Michael Kava in my time. You see the youth of today, filling stadiums, worshipping singers. Others, rioting at universities. This is a decaying generation.'

'What is your opinion of President Zara?'

'He has wings.'

'What did he mean?' Salman reflected. Ambitious? A Caesar who would be murdered?

'You know I am a prisoner in a democratic state. You are fortunate. You are a jailer.'

He laughed. Salman froze.

'I am glad you are no longer in charge of education. From Monday to Friday teachers are drinking, seducing lady teachers, schoolgirls. Have you seen the television series, *Classroom Frolics*? The Minister says it's educational. A nation seeing itself. Reformation will follow. What rubbish! I should have stopped you giving teachers more money, housing allowances, medical aid. I worked underground. From hard work comes gold. You have the right portfolio. Lock them up. Starve them.'

'I must go now.'

'No. You must have tea with me. I don't know when you will come again.'

He rang a bell that stood on a small table before him and two maids came in with tea and confectionery.

He enjoyed two tarts with his tea and his visitor, a cream pastry.

'Salman, here I am in a mansion. Sentry at the gate, maids, chauffeur, Rolls Royce. Have you seen a hawk in the zoo? I am like that bird. Confined, as good as dead.'

He wiped his lips and hands with a serviette and said:

'A few days ago I recorded a Turkish tale I heard over the radio. I translated and transcribed it yesterday. It is very relevant to our times. I would like to read it to you.'

He went to a display cabinet, opened a drawer at the bottom, returned with the script and read:

THE STATUE

The old man came every day to sit in the park in front of the Palace of Congress. He would sit on a bench not far from the statue of President Hasub. The giant statue of the President stood on a wide circular platform with stone steps from opposite sides leading up to it. The statue had been there for a decade after the President's death, looking across an avenue flanked by oak trees. The park was a place of palms, jacaranda trees and frangipani shrubs near fountains and parterres that looked very colourful in the sunlight.

One morning he saw a crane and a ten-wheeled truck near the statue. There was a man seated in the control box of the crane. Workmen had climbed up the steps to the statue and seemed to be harnessing it with chains. He went near the man in the control box and waved at him to come down.

'I want to have a word with you,' he shouted.

'What for?'

'Come down and you will know.'

The man, who was very short and in blue uniform, climbed down the steel steps and, when he reached the ground was asked, 'Can you explain why you are removing the statue?'

'I have orders from President Zadek's office.'

'I don't know about the order and don't want it removed.'

'Then you will have to speak to the President. But tell me, why don't you want it removed?'

'Because the man was evil.'

'All the more reason for removing his statue.'

'No. President Hasub's statue should remain here to remind us of his misdeeds.'

'I don't know of any he committed.'

'Then you don't know history. He ordered his army to invade the lands of the Koras, the Hitis and the Rojas, commit genocide and annex them.'

'Perhaps President Zadek has realised that President Hasub was indeed an evil man and has decided to order the statue removed.'

'You are mistaken. President Zadek wants to be remembered by posterity, and while this statue stands here he cannot feel at ease. That is the way of rulers. They always want to destroy history so that they alone are remembered, especially for conducting successful wars.'

'That may be true or not true. As far as I am concerned I have to carry out higher orders.'

The workmen on the platform shouted that they were ready. The crane operator quickly climbed the steps to his control box. The crane's arm was lowered, and a chain with a steel hook came down and was linked with the chained statue. The statue was lifted, placed on the truck, and soon crane, truck and President Hasub were gone.

He did not visit the park again for several months because of ill-health, and therefore did not see the new statue, that of President Zadek, on the platform. On the day he died, President Zadek declared war against the citizens of the nearby island of Fara "for overthrowing King Atun who was a loyal friend of the democratic free world".

'A good story and well read,' Salman praised. 'If you had married you would not have been lonely today.'

'I didn't want to rear children in Apartheid times. I am glad I have none to be corrupted in this age. Have you seen school pupils and striking workers marching through city streets, destroying, looting from shops and hawkers? I visited Germany, Poland, Bulgaria. The people there know what work is. In parliament now they cry: "We want our land back from the white farmers." But give them a spade, a fork. They won't plant a bean.'

Salman stood up to leave.

'Stay a while longer. You have done so much. The others, when they are criticised? O, there is the Apartheid legacy to overcome. In the struggle we argued, disagreed, criticised and worked together.'

'Yes, the times were different.'

'Now conference after conference. Commonwealth Conference, United Africa Conference, Renaissance Conference. And banquets, banquets. Consider history. The whites, when they conquered, they were lean, strong, alert. What happened next? Rich, fat, torpid, can't fight, want reconciliation. Now the new rich. What will be their end? You know. You are a professor.'

'You are not hopeful of the future?'

'Have you seen the leaders of the world's so-called democracies? Presidents, prime ministers, diplomats? Adolescents all. There is no Caesar, Geronimo, Samson, Saladin.'

'Is that why you resigned?'

'When I resigned there was speculation. Generous, leaving country to young men. Tired. Old. Wants to write memoirs. Now you know. Report me correctly when I am gone.'

Salman again stood up to leave.

'Before you go, come with me to the back garden.'

Salman followed him.

They emerged from a back door and walked along a winding path on either side of which flourished vegetables of all kinds.

He stopped, stretched his hands out on both sides, to the east and west, and said: 'This is my treasure, my joy.'

Salman saw nothing to be proud of in a vegetable garden.

An assistant was watering the beds. He beckoned to him and when he came up said, 'Bring me a box.'

The man ran to a shed and returned with one.

'Come,' he said to Salman, 'take some fresh vegetables home. Elizabeth will appreciate them.'

He selected aubergines, green and red peppers, lettuces, carrots, watercress, cucumbers, radish, spinach, beetroot.

'All grown with natural organic fertiliser, Salman. Good for your health. You must be strong to face the future.'

He told his assistant to take the box to the car at the gate. He and Salman followed.

His farewell words were: 'Give my love to Elizabeth. And when you come again bring me a video of John Wayne, will you.'

He smiled and waved at Salman until the car turned a corner.

When the car came to a stop at the airport entrance, Salman paid the taxi man and said, 'You can have the vegetables.'

'Are you certain, sir? I have never seen such lovely greens.'

'Take them home and give them to your wife. She will appreciate them.'

In the airport lounge Salman felt bitter. He had erred in visiting. The man lived in the past, in the age of film heroes. He had no understanding of his fall from the Education portfolio. In fact he saw it as a promotion. He imagined himself to be a hero. John Wayne indeed! He would go on deluding himself and end by buying a horse and riding through the streets of East London, a ridiculous antiquated figure. Don Quixote.

XXIX

ONE SATURDAY AFTERNOON Mr Khamsin telephoned Salman and said that three muftis of the Islamic Council had asked him to arrange an interview with him. They wished to discuss various matters, especially relating to legislation that contravened Islamic social law.

He recalled the delegation sent by Mr Bengali. He had been riled by their arrogance and would not like to be involved in religious altercation with theologians. He told this to Mr Khamsin who said that the muftis had no requests to make but to get his opinion.

'If you are present I will see them.'

'I will make myself available. I will fetch them and bring them to your home this evening,' he agreed.

They came in the evening and Mr Khamsin introduced them. They were dressed in long coats, buttoned to the neck, and wore white turbans. They salaamed and shook hands.

'Professor Sahib,' Mufti Suleiman began, 'you know there are many casinos being built all over the country and we are getting worried. Our youth are being attracted by gambling. Can you suggest anything we can do?'

'You must tell the youth in the seminaries and mosques that these places are forbidden to them.'

'We are doing that, but every week-end the casinos are full. There are also other entertainments provided in casino buildings such as half-naked dancing and entire families are going there.'

'I don't think one can ask the government to close them. They are part of business, they create work for many. You know we have a very high unemployment rate in the country. They also attract tourists. There is only one answer. Educate the community.'

'They are institutions of the kafirun to destroy us,' the second Mufti declared.

'That may be so if you let them. But we should not use insulting terms.'

'That is not an insulting term. It means non-believers.'

Mr Khamsin intervened.

'Mufti Ebrahim, what we consider to have a factual meaning can be interpreted as insulting by others. We must be careful.'

'Mufti Ebrahim,' Salman addressed him. 'We are a small minority in this country and we cannot object to what the majority wants. We can only resort to educating our youth and parents.'

'There are ten Muslims,' Mufti Suleiman said, 'in parliament, but they don't say a word about all the evil that goes on. Besides gambling there is prostitution, drinking, adultery, sodomy, abortion.'

'We cannot,' Mr Khamsin emphasised, 'because what we say will be set aside by the majority. It is better to be silent than create enemies.'

'I see your point, brother Ismail. But what about our beliefs. We must state them whether they like them or not. It is our Islamic obligation.'

'I understand. In a different society and a different time one could. We have just come out of the Apartheid era when many of our people were uprooted from homes and shops – to this day Fourteenth Street in Pageview is a wreck. We will have to be patient. Many changes have been made and many will still come, some of them very unpleasant. We must continue to preserve our traditions and our wonderful way of life. As the professor sahib has said, the answer lies in education.'

'Another thing,' Mufti Suleiman went on, 'why is the government not locking up drug dealers? Some Muslims are selling these haram things to our children.'

Salman attempted a reply: 'You have seen on television … '

'I don't watch television. It is evil.'

'Then you must have read in our newspapers how drug-couriers have been arrested at our airports. Cocaine, mandrax tablets by the million have been confiscated.'

'Drug dealers in our community are not arrested. Can you explain why?'

'You have read what is happening in Cape Town. There is a war going on.'

'No, we don't need that.'

'Professor Sahib,' Mufti Ebrahim said, 'the government has recognised gays. They can even marry.'

'This state is a secular one. It does not take religion as a guide.'

'The Muslims in parliament should be guides.'

'We will be called "fundamentalists" and "terrorists".'

'Mufti Ebrahim,' Mr Khamsin addressed him, 'we must realise that the world with the coming of television is no longer the same. Words cannot change people any longer.'

'What about Aids? Many people are dying.'

'We must tell our children that if they follow Islam they will be safe. If the others wish to die we cannot stop them. Let them dance, sing, commit sodomy and adultery. Those who survive will become Muslims.' There was agreement from the Muftis.

The visitors went on to discuss other matters: liquor, the state lottery, usury by commercial banks. Before they left, Mufti Mohammed who had remained silent throughout the discussion said:

'Professor Sahib, one day when you are president we shall have a good government.'

XXX

THE STATEMENT BY THE THIRD MUFTI that he would be the president one day convinced Salman that he was the man destiny had chosen. The third prophecy would inevitably move towards fulfillment. It now became imperative for him to visit Mr Roma. During his visit he would finally know whether he was the man the prophet had in mind.

Had he not sat next to him during the television discussion? His sibylline insight must have intuitively communicated to him that the man next to him would bring light after the dark phase. The dark phase had a double meaning: it meant not only the descent of the country into the marsh of economic stagnation and social decay, but his own descent into the murk of prisons. The final phase would be his ascent to the highest position in the state. But when would that happen? What changes would have to occur in the consciousness of the citizens and in the body politic for a Muslim to be elected president? The proletariat were still an ignorant mass, and the new middle class, like the whites, conditioned by the materialistic ethos of the West. He had reverted to the religion into which he was born and by that act placed himself in the hands of the Omnipotent to guide him to his august destiny. Was he not a descendant of the great royal khans?

The next day he looked for Mr Roma's name in the telephone directory. There were seven others with the same name. He thought of the television station. They would have his address and telephone number. He asked Allison to find out, which she did.

He spoke to Mr Roma who said that he would be very happy to renew the acquaintance. He gave him directions to his home in the country.

After he replaced the telephone on its cradle he began to have doubts. The man might be an impostor. If he discovered this what would be the consequence? His hope of rising from his hateful portfolio would be dashed. What would he do then? Did the witches not betray Macbeth? He recalled the warrior's doubts:

> And oftentimes, to win us to our harm,
> The instruments of darkness tell us truths,
> Win us with honest trifles, to betray's
> In deepest consequence.

After wrestling mentally with himself, he decided to undertake the journey to the prophet. He must know the truth. Indecision would place him on the rack.

On a Sunday he set out in his car. After about two hours he reached the town of Rossburg, passed through Main street, then went on until he saw a sign showing Ridgeway. He turned onto a gravel road and travelled for about four kilometres until he reached a large white-painted house architecturally designed in the Cape Dutch style, with gables and window shutters. The gate was an wrought-iron structure on either side of which, at regular intervals, were short pillars on which were ornamental pots.

On the left of the house was an orange grove; on the right vegetable gardens where men and women were digging with hoes. Further away there was a cluster of thatch-roofed huts shaded by trees below several ridges where tall aloes were to be seen among bronze boulders. Cattle were grazing in a fenced enclosure.

Mr Roma came to the gate to welcome his visitor.

'I am pleased you have arrived safely.'

'You have a peaceful place here. This is where you receive inspiration.'

Mr Roma was dressed in a similar garment to the one he wore during the television discussion, but emerald in colour. His complexion was tawny, hair curly and glossy, his face smooth and his frame athletic. He led Salman to the entrance door and into the reception room. There were two settees, several armchairs, glass cabinets with pots decorated with geometrical patterns, and flowers in vases.

They sat down.

'I enjoyed listening to you in the television studio,' Salman began. 'What you said was very interesting.'

'It was a pleasure to meet you, Dr Khan.'

'Where were you educated?'

'I went to a mission school and later studied for a BA degree by correspondence with the University of South Africa in Pretoria.'

'That was an achievement in the previous era.'

'Some people think that no one received tertiary education in that era.'

'I attended university here and then went to Cambridge to acquire a doctorate in Medieval history.'

'I studied history and religions.'

'Then both of us have an interest in history.'

A young woman in a dark blue skirt, a cream blouse and a beaded necklace entered with a tray on which were two glasses and a jug containing orange juice. She placed the tray on a small table, then turned to Salman and curtsied.

'My daughter, Zimi,' Mr Roma introduced her.

Salman acknowledged her curtsy by saying, 'She is lovely.' He admired her lithe form.

She left.

Mr Roma poured two glasses of orange juice and handed one to his guest.

'Your place is tranquil,' Salman praised. 'I wish I lived here instead of in a suburb.'

'One cannot reflect in a city.'

'Yes, the hurly-burly distracts.'

Two women came in. They were both wearing full skirts and chiffon scarves.

'My wives.' Salman stood up and they curtsied. He noticed that they were slender, unlike the bulbous women in parliament and in cities. They seemed to be imbued with natural dignity, serenity and grace.

When they left Salman said with a slight tremor in his voice:

'Mr Roma, do you recall the prophecy you made in the television studio? The third one. You said that this country would one day have a Muslim president.'

'Religions have a great deal to teach us.'

'There is also much to learn from history.'

'That too, as well as the present.'

'You made two other prophecies that have been fulfilled. You said a star would set and the President resigned. You also said the country would pass through a dark phase and that is what I see happening now.'

'That was easy to tell. The President had had a long political career and could not go on very much longer. And the ruling party's administrative record gave me no confidence.'

'Was the third prophecy ... '

'Call it prediction.'

'Was it based on intuition?'

'Not all intuitions are genuine intuitions. Sometimes a wish comes in the semblance of an intuition.'

'A wish?'

'When things are not going well, we wish that a great personality would come to introduce a new age, and the wish takes on the semblance of an intuition.'

Salman remained silent.

'You know,' Mr Roma went on, 'Islam is a faith that does not separate the secular and the sacred. And a principal tenet of Islam is social justice. And how can we have social justice in a state when rulers are guided by secular values? Election to office is not a gift but a moral responsibility. When politicians and bureaucrats realise this we shall have a good state.'

'What interests me is how did you come to the conclusion that a Muslim would be president in the future?'

'Do you know, doctor, that I have met a Muslim who said that he was the expected Mahdi of the new millennium.'

'I have not heard of anyone making that claim.'

'All religions, including the teachings of Lao Tzu and Confucius, warn us that obsessive pursuit of material values will lead us astray. Only when the secular and sacred are integrated and harmonised will we have a world without conflict and cruelty. States that are secular are based on the shifting sands of relative values. As long as ethics remain beyond the acts of politicians, there shall be no peace and happiness.'

Salman felt disappointed, but concealed it as best he could. He had not come there to listen to a sermon.

After some further talk unrelated to the prophecy, Salman decided to leave.

'I am pleased you have come. Many politicians have no interest in traditional wisdom.'

As they walked out towards the car, Mr Roma's wives came with two stringbags of oranges.

'Take these as a gift.'

Salman opened the boot of his car. The oranges were placed within. The women curtsied and left.

'Thanks very much, Mr Roma.'

'Go well and take care. We live in troubled times.'

On his way home he crossed a bridge, stopped the car and emerged. He walked despondently towards the bridge, stood beside the concrete balustrade and looked into the turbid water. A sense of loneliness and misery clutched him. He had come to meet the prophet with hope and it had been shattered. Macbeth's words regarding the veracity of the witches surfaced in his memory:

> And be these juggling fiends no more believed,
> That palter with us in a double sense;
> That keep the word of promise to our ear,
> And break it to our hope.

When he returned to his car he opened the boot and looked at the oranges. Could he enjoy them without thinking of Mr

Roma's evasiveness on the third prophecy? Should he throw them into the river or leave them along the roadside? He took out the two stringbags and left them next to the road.

As he drove on he felt he had been ungrateful to Mr Roma's wives. They had presented oranges to him and curtsied with respect. He turned his car and returned to the bridge. When he got there the oranges were gone. Someone had taken them.

He drove home, carrying within him a profound sense of loss.

That night he sat on the balcony of his mansion, looked up at the stars, saw Jupiter's brilliant jewel and thought of his act of leaving the oranges along the roadside. Mr Roma had uttered a great truth, that of observing an ethical imperative in human acts, and he had failed to appreciate the import. What could be more unethical than to spurn the fruit of the earth, fruit that had been grown with care and devotion by him, his wives and his lovely daughter? He had stained himself by his ingratitude. Not all the perfumes of Arabia …

XXXI

O N SUNDAYS SALMAN USUALLY went to the shops north of Houghton to buy newspapers: *The Weekly Mail, The Sunday Independent* and *The Sunday Times*. One Sunday he decided to buy the papers in Fordsburg. When he had accompanied Mr Khamsin to the Mayfair Mosque he had passed through Mint Road and seen cafés there.

When he reached Fordsburg he parked his Mercedes near two train coaches that had been converted into a restaurant called the Orient Express. He decided to have a closer look. He walked around the coaches on rails, and when he stood before the entrance steps he saw that the front resembled a Victorian station. He walked up the steps, flanked by flowering shrubs, and entered the foyer. On either side were the coaches and within, dining tables with the original seats.

A stair on the left led to an upper level where there were other dining tables. A lady in a sari came up to him, and said courteously: 'Can I help you, sir?'

'I am admiring the structure of the restaurant. It must be unique.'

'Yes, and the menu is also unique. You must try it some time.'

'I think I will this evening.'

He had not entered a train coach since his arrival in the country and decided that he would come with Elizabeth. He would also invite Mr Khamsin, his wives and all his children. They would enjoy dining in an unusual restaurant. The lady accompanied him to the entrance and bade him good day.

He walked around the coaches again. They had been painted in the original brown colour of yesteryear and the chrome and brass handles gleamed. Between the rails were dark wood sleepers and grey stones.

Salman crossed the road and bought the newspapers at a café. He returned to his car, opened the door and placed the papers within. He was about to enter when he felt a hard instrument pushed into his back and heard a voice threaten: 'Give me the key or you'll be dead.'

Another figure loomed on his left, hemming him in. He gave the key, shocked and bewildered. The man entered the car. He found himself pushed into the rear seat with a man sitting beside him. The car moved away.

The entire incident happened so quickly that he lost his sense of time and place. The car took a turn with screeching wheels and sped on. For a moment he had the illusion that he was sitting in the coach of the Orient Express and the buildings on either side were hurtling past at speed. After several more turns he awakened to reality and realised he had been hijacked.

'Take the car and let me get off,' he pleaded.

Neither the man who sat beside him with his heavy arm over his shoulder nor the man driving the car spoke.

'Please ... take the car ... take the money.'

'Give it,' the man next to him said. He put his hand into his rear trouser pocket and gave him a wad of notes.

'Now let me go.'

'No,' the man said, taking the notes and counting them.

'More.'

'I have no more.'

'We kill you today.' The man replaced his arm around his shoulder and pressed him down.

Fear seized him. He prayed, would repent, go to Mecca, dispense charity, fast.

Time stretched to eternity.

The car stopped suddenly and he lurched forward. The arm was thrown off him. A door opened. Another man got in. The third murderer. Banquo. Murderers closing in. ''Tis he.' 'Let it come down.' Terror and panic fused experiences, events, memories, words into surreal hallucinations. He was in a hurtling train, bridges collapsing into flooding rivers, Madam Nomsa bat Hecate in dining carriage eating eye of newt and toe of frog Fortune Queens dancing round cauldron boil and bubble toil and trouble prison doors flying open multitudes fleeing through streets of flaming cars Shaykh Sayid with scimitar upraised rushing towards headless Macbeth naked Allison screaming in dungeon of howling reptiles women in black veils circling above Table Mountain President John Wayne at window on black stallion galloping into desert of stone obelisks women on roadside with orange dresses beckoning and ascending to constellations.

The car stopped Robot Shop fronts Billboards Neon signs Church steeple. The oppressive arm Kill today Stab shoot bludgeon hang no don't please! please! Screaming engine rushing wind roaring road screeching halt. Out! Out! pushed fell lost consciousness.

When he revived he sat up and looked at the surroundings. He was sitting on a pavement. On his right were buildings. On his left columns of trees and a lake. He stood up, his body aching. He walked slowly towards the lake and saw two figures seated on a bench. He went towards them.

'I need help,' he said.

The couple stood up quickly.

'You are hurt,' the man said.

'I have been hijacked.'

They saw congealing blood on his forehead, nose and left cheek. His shirt was torn and his left shoulder bloody.

'Come home with us,' the lady said. 'You need attention.'

'Do you have a cell phone?'

'Yes, in the car. Harold, fetch it.'

The man ran to the nearby car park.

'I have an orange drink,' the lady said. 'Sit down.'

She opened a wicker basket, poured the drink into a glass and gave it to him.

'Thank you. What place is this?'

'Florida.'

The man came with the cellphone.

He telephoned Elizabeth, told her what had happened, where he was, and said that she should come with Mr Khamsin. Then he related to the couple his ordeal.

'You are extremely lucky,' the man said. 'Many are killed as criminals don't want to be identified if caught.'

Mr Khamsin arrived with Elizabeth. Salman introduced them to the couple who had helped him, asked Mr Khamsin to record their names and address, thanked them and entered the Daimler.

On the way home he recounted what had happened.

'You must thank the Almighty,' Mr Khamsin said.

That he accepted. He had been saved by divine intervention. Many reports of hijackings had appeared in newspapers over the years. Women had been gang-raped and murdered.

At home a doctor was called. He examined Salman and tended his wounds. After lunch Mr Khamsin said:

'Let us go to the police station now and report the matter. And we must inform the newspapers.'

'We have to return to Cape Town tomorrow.'

'You must stay at home for a few days to recover.'

'I prefer to remain silent.'

'A crime has to be reported. The country must know. None of us is safe.'

'How could they do this to me?'

'It can happen to anyone, Salman.'

'But why me?'

'Two provincial ministers were hijacked last year and they were pushed into the boots of their cars. You remember? Recently a lady's car was not only taken from her home, but she was killed by the robbers who drove over her.'

'But why me?' he asked again, unable to bear the humiliation.

'Since the death sentence was abolished we are all vulnerable.'

The two men went to the police station.

That night Salman slept uneasily. He woke up several times. He dreamt of a speeding express train that rattled, shook, went off the rails and plunged down a precipice into a lake.

In the morning newspaper reporters arrived. The afternoon newspapers carried the sensational news of the hijacking of a Cabinet Minister, the man responsible for keeping criminals under lock and key. There was a statement by him: 'The administration must give priority to the safety and security of citizens. That is the principal reason for the establishment of states. South Africa is gaining notoriety for its violence. If firm action is not taken, the country will descend into anarchy with serious consequences for the economy.'

Later, Shareef, Kamar, Zenobia and others came to offer consolation.

When Salman returned to his office the next day, he was welcomed back by the President, ministers and members of parliament, with the exception of Mr Bengali.

Allison was very pleased to see him.

'You have been saved for me,' she said, holding his hand.

She handed him a telegram from the first President which read:

'You are safe Salman and that is all I need to know.'

In the evening Mr Khamsin said to him: 'You should not have made that statement to the press on crime. The President might interpret it as an indictment.'

'Let him. When we are victims then only do we see the reality. I shall never forget the experience. How can anyone subject another human being to such a harrowing ride in his own car. Only in a country that has descended into evil can this happen. I wish I had never returned.'

'There is crime all over the world.'

'Not to this extent. Look at our statistics. They meant nothing to me until this happened. When it happens to others our feelings are not involved. When evil stretches its hand to us then we know its true nature.'

At supper time Salman said to Mr Khamsin:

'I must give a thousand to the couple who assisted at the lake.'

'A thousand!'

151

'When you have experienced what I have, then you will know what it is to find two human beings who do all they can to provide comfort.'

The next day Salman received the following letter from Saleem Anwar Sayid:

'I read the report of your experience with criminals in *The Cape Herald*. By the Grace of Allah you were saved. The mercy you extended to those in need was bestowed on you by the Omnipotent. All praise to Him! You will now more fully appreciate that the struggle against evil in our society must continue, if necessary until the Final Hour. My salaams to you and your family.'

Salman's ride with the hijackers remained an incubus in his memory. He would wake fearfully at night after surreal dreams. Several times a Cyclopean arm lay heavily over his shoulder and compressed him until he felt he was near death. Once he dreamt he was a prisoner of Ebrahim driving recklessly through a winding storm-drenched pass. Stopping suddenly, he leapt out of the car, screamed hysterically with gun in hand for him to come out, and shot himself as lightning flashed. At times, sitting at his desk in his office, he would remain transfixed with pen uplifted. In the council chamber he would not be listening to the debates and only come out of his abstracted state when acrid words were exchanged.

He bought another car, but not a Mercedes. The police later located its burnt remains on a country road. In his imagination he saw the hijackers setting fire to it gleefully, the flames devouring it and the smoke floating away over a tranquil landscape.

XXXII

AFTER THE PASSAGE OF SEVERAL MONTHS, reports appeared in newspapers that the President contemplated changes in the Cabinet. He was unhappy with the performance of some Ministers. There was much speculation about who he was going to drop from the legislature and who he was going to promote. Ministers removed from their posts would remain members of parliament.

Salman became despondent and apprehensive. He remembered the occasions when he went into the President's office and the cavalier way he had been treated.

'I think he is going to axe me,' he told Elizabeth.

'Why think? Wait and see.'

'I will be an ordinary MP.'

'You will still earn a salary.'

'What consolation will that be when I am demoted.'

'Salman, forget what he will do. You agonised enough when he took your Education portfolio away.'

'The newspapers were on my side then. Will they support me if I am axed?'

'Of course. You have handled the overcrowding in prisons very well.'

'Yes, I must not allow what he will do to make me miserable.'

When he told Allison of his fear of losing his ministerial position, she said;

'If that happens it will not separate us.'

'A prophet predicted these dark times.'

'A prophet?'

'He said that this country would pass through a dark phase.'

'Who is this prophet and when did he say that?'

He told her.

'But I am not exempted. These dark times include me.'

'Don't be pessimistic. If the President removes you, you will be remembered for the good work you have done.'

153

'I have always done my best. He did not appreciate my work in education and gave me the Prison portfolio.'

'If he cannot appreciate you then he will fall some day.'

'Fall, Allison?'

'Yes. Why should he not fall when many others have who lacked good judgment? And you will regain your position in the Cabinet and later rise higher.'

The third prophecy! Even his secretary in some occult way referred to it. Though Mr Roma had concealed from him the name of the future president, he felt hopeful that events would still move favourably in his direction. Two truths had come to realisation. The star. The dark phase. The third was inevitable. But as the days passed his optimism wilted and the certainty that he would be dismissed settled like slag within him.

When he told Mr Khamsin of his fear, he advised:

'Do not panic. He may drop you or he may not. He may move you to another portfolio or he may not. If he drops you, you will still be in parliament and be relieved of much work. You have over extended yourself and some rest will do you good.'

President Zara announced his revised Cabinet.

Salman was dropped.

Mr Khamsin was appointed as Minister of Trade and Industry.

'Don't be upset,' Mr Khamsin sympathised. 'You may be appointed later again. Your post as Minister of Prisons was always beneath you. Besides, you should be pleased as you are now released from dealing with Shaykh Sayid. You don't know where that could have led you.'

'Tell me, do you think there is a determined pattern in what happens in life? That what I have experienced is meaningful?'

'The Qur'an tells us that God did not create the world in sport.'

He did not feel comforted. He ardently wished he had stayed in the lecture halls of Cambridge and never returned. Here was Mr Khamsin, a man who had not attended university. He had ascended while he, Salman, had fallen. He had played no part in the liberation struggle, in fact had enriched himself in Apartheid times. Now he was a Cabinet Minister. He was not only a master of commerce but a man who knew how to arrange things to his advantage.

That night, in his bedroom in the Diaz Hotel, he felt wretched and lonely. He could not sleep. Then it occurred to him, like a revelation, that Mr Khamsin was the man destiny had chosen to be the future president. He was a devout Muslim, buoyant in temperament, keenly perceptive of political realities, diplomatic in his relationship with others, prudent in making statements, calculating in action, convincing in argument. Above all he possessed the energy to advance towards whatever he wished to achieve.

Saturated with anguish, his essence permanently violated by his reduction, Salman recalled Macbeth's soliloquy after the death of the queen, a soliloquy that had etched itself on the tablet of his memory and that of many pupils during his youth. Recalling the final words with their despair-laden nihilism his eyes closed in sleep:

> ... it is a tale
> Told by an idiot, full of sound and fury,
> Signifying nothing.

When Salman returned home on Friday he felt ill, mentally and physically. He would now be conscious of his humiliation every day of his life. In the council chamber that viper, Mr Bengali, would stare at him ironically, taking delight in his fall. He was a prisoner with one exit open to him – he must resign. He told Elizabeth of his intention.

'Why do you want to throw away your salary? We have a beautiful home to maintain.'

'I don't care about the salary or this home. The President has treated me as a commodity of no consequence, like the hijackers.'

'The newspapers have been critical of your removal.'

'That does not reduce my humiliation.'
'Your distinguished academic status will remain intact.'
'Distinguished did you say? O Elizabeth!'
He turned pale, had difficulty in breathing, and collapsed.